D0057621

Sudden Death in New York City

Roy MacGregor

M&S

An M&S Paperback Original from
McClelland & Stewart Ltd.
The Canadian Publishers

For editor Alex Schultz, guardian of the Owls, with gratitude

The author is grateful to Doug Gibson, who thought up this series.

An M&S Paperback Original from McClelland & Stewart Ltd.

Copyright © 2000 by Roy MacGregor

All rights reserved. The use of any part of this publication reproduced, transmitted in any form or by any means, electronic, mechanical, photocopying, recording, or otherwise, or stored in a retrieval system, without the prior written consent of the publisher – or, in case of photocopying or other reprographic copying, a licence from the Canadian Copyright Licensing Agency – is an infringement of the copyright law.

Canadian Cataloguing in Publication Data

MacGregor, Roy, 1948–
    Sudden death in New York City

(The Screech Owls series; 13)
ISBN 0-7710-5642-7

I. Title. II. Series: MacGregor, Roy, 1948– . Screech Owls series.

PS8575.G84S92 2000   jC813'.54   C00-932194-2
PZ7.M1463Su 2000

We acknowledge the financial support of the Government of Canada through the Book Publishing Industry Development Program for our publishing activities. We further acknowledge the support of the Canada Council for the Arts and the Ontario Arts Council for our publishing program.

Cover illustration by Gregory C. Banning
Typeset in Bembo by M&S, Toronto

Printed and bound in Canada

McClelland & Stewart Ltd.
The Canadian Publishers
481 University Avenue
Toronto, Ontario
M5G 2E9
www.mcclelland.com

2 3 4 5 04 03 02

1

"FINGERNAILS?" FAHD SUGGESTED.

"For-*get* it!" Nish snorted. "I *chew* mine."

"It would take too long, anyway," mumbled Fahd, his head almost buried in the large book he held open over his shinpads. "World record for the longest fingernail . . ." Fahd looked up, his eyes widening, ". . . is four feet, one-and-a-half inches!"

"How the heck would you pick your nose?" Nish asked.

Most of the Screech Owls laughed. Travis Lindsay just shook his head. Wayne Nishikawa had always been, at one and the same time, the person he knew best and the person he knew least.

They had gone to kindergarten together, taken karate lessons together, played on the same soccer, baseball, and, of course, hockey teams. They had been in the same class every year but one. Weekends, when Travis wasn't sleeping over at Nish's house, Nish was usually sleeping over at Travis's. And yet, despite all those years, despite all those opportunities to see Nish's mind at work, Travis never had any idea what was going to come out of his best friend's mouth. Only that it would be crazy – and that someone had better laugh or else Nish would come out with something even more insane.

It was getting stuffy in the dressing room at the Tamarack Memorial Arena. The Owls were ready for practice, but the local junior team had run overtime, and the big players had left the ice so choppy and rutted that Mr. Dillinger, the Owls' manager, had begged the arena staff for a double flood. The Zamboni was only now beginning its second round.

Fahd had his *Guinness Book of World Records* out while they waited. Even though they were just days away from setting out by bus for New York City and the Big Apple International Peewee Tournament, every one of them was thinking about Nish and his New Year's resolution instead of the practice ahead.

How does Nish do it? Travis wondered. How does he pull everyone into his crazy little world? How does one chubby, goofy-looking twelve-year-old manage to be the centre of attention, no matter what?

They were leaving Tamarack on December 27, the day after Boxing Day. They would be in New York for New Year's Eve, and their coach, Muck Munro, and the team manager, Mr. Dillinger, had promised they could stay up until midnight and attend the celebrations in Times Square – *so long as they behaved themselves.*

Where Nish got the idea of getting his name into the *Guinness Book of World Records*, Travis couldn't be sure. It hadn't come from reading, he was pretty certain of that. If something wasn't on television, if it wasn't on the Internet or in a new video game or the latest movie, Nish didn't even know it existed.

But somewhere he had come up with this hare-brained notion that he could get himself into the *Guinness Book of World Records*. He'd almost driven the team crazy with it.

He'd started out thinking he'd score more goals than any minor-hockey player in history. But Willie Granger, the team's hockey trivia expert, had put a quick end to that ambition. "Wayne Gretzky had 378 one year as a novice," Willie had pointed out.

"I'm peewee," Nish had protested.

Willie had shaken his head. "He had 196 goals the year he was twelve, same age as you. I don't think you could score 170 goals between now and the end of the season – not even in practice."

Now, with the New York tournament less than a week off, Nish had almost the entire team searching out ideas for him. Fahd had offered up a dozen or more from the *Guinness Book of World Records*, including the ridiculous one of Nish, the nail biter, growing the world's longest fingernails.

"Here's a guy in Kentucky who ate sixty-eight dew worms in thirty seconds," said Fahd.

"*And then hurled for three hours!*" laughed Nish.

"How about stupid penalties?" Sarah shouted from the far side of the room. "You take enough of them, that's for sure."

Nish paused only for a quick flick of his tongue in her direction. Then he turned to Data. "What's the NHL record?"

Data had his *National Hockey League Official Guide and Record Book* on his lap, the cover resting on an arm of his wheelchair as he flipped through the thick volume with one hand. "Dave Williams," Data announced. "That's 'Tiger' Williams. Three thousand, nine hundred and sixty-six minutes . . . That's, let me see . . . just over sixty-six hours in the penalty box . . . six hours short of three full days."

Nish winced. "How about for one season?"

Data read again. "Dave Schultz – the 'Hammer.' Four hundred and seventy-two minutes . . . That's just short of eight hours."

"Muck'd kill you," shouted Sam, sitting beside Sarah.

Nish slumped unhappily in his seat. "I gotta find *something!*"

The team was well used to Nish's little funks, and they completely ignored him as talk turned to other matters. Lars Johansson wouldn't be coming, as he was spending the holidays with his grandparents in Sweden. Mario Terziano, who'd played several previous tournaments with the

Owls, was being brought in to replace Lars. Everyone else was coming. Jesse Highboy was hoping for one of Mr. Dillinger's famous Stupid Stops on the bus trip to New York, when Mr. Dillinger would hand out dollars and insist that they "buy something absolutely useless with it." Derek Dillinger made a joke about "wedgies," and Dmitri Yakushev wondered if they'd be seeing the Statue of Liberty.

"Times Square is going to be the big thing," said Jenny Staples, the backup goaltender. "There might be a million people there."

"And more than a *billion* watching on TV," added Fahd.

"They'll have the countdown on that big screen in Times Square," said Derek. "I think it might be the biggest in the world."

Nish came suddenly alert. He sat up sharply, his face flushing with excitement. "How many?" he asked Fahd.

"A *billion*, I think."

"It's televised?"

"All over the world. You've seen it. Everybody's seen the countdown."

"Live?" Nish asked, his face gleaming.

"Of course live, you idiot," shouted Sam, looking up from retying her skates. "It's the countdown for the New Year. You think they tape it and play it the next day?"

Everyone laughed, but not Nish.

"Live? One *billion* people watching?"

"Yeah," said Sarah. "So?"

"So," Nish said triumphantly, turning on Fahd. "Is there anything in the *Guinness Book of World Records* on 'mooning'?"

Fahd looked up, incredulous. "*What?*"

"*Mooning* — what's the world's record for mooning? If I mooned a billion people at once, would I get in?"

Travis looked across the room at Sarah, who rolled her eyes and sighed.

Travis tried to cut off his imagination, but it had already raced ahead of him. He could see the crowd at Times Square. He could see the big video monitor and hear the countdown: *Ten!* . . . *Nine!* . . . *Eight!* . . . *Seven!* . . . *Six!* . . . *Five!* . . . *Four!* . . . *Three!* . . . *Two!* . . . *One!* And then, instead of the fireworks and balloons, the big screen filling with the bare-naked butt of the world's craziest peewee hockey player. Travis shook his head hard, hoping to shake off the thought the way a wet dog throws off water.

"Would I get in?" Nish repeated.

"Well, I guess," said Fahd. "But you'd get in big trouble, wouldn't you?"

"How?" Nish laughed, as if Fahd had just asked the dumbest question ever. "It's not as if I'd be sticking my *face* on the screen, is it?"

2

THEY DROVE DOWN TO NEW YORK IN A LIGHT, wet snow that turned the pavement ahead black and glistening. Mr. Dillinger drove the old bus, sticking to the turnpikes and stopping only for bathroom breaks and lunch. He kept the music low, the heavy beat of the windshield wipers droning over everything, and soon most of the bus was asleep. Muck dozed in the seat closest to the door, a big book slipping off his lap several times as he fell into a deep slumber. Sam and Sarah slept with their heads tilted together. Fahd and Data played games on Data's new laptop computer until the battery ran down, and then they too slept. All up and down the old bus there were legs sticking out in the aisle, pillows jammed against windows, jackets over heads.

Travis got up at one point to stretch his legs. He looked towards the back of the bus, where much of the Screech Owls' equipment had been piled in the empty seats. There was a window on the safety door at the back, and he thought he might just stand there awhile and watch the traffic.

Unfortunately, someone was already there.

Nish. His back to the window. Bent over almost double. His belt undone and pants down around his ankles.

"*What are you doing?*" Travis hissed.

Nish looked up, blinked a couple of times as if the answer were obvious. "Practising."

"*Practising?*" Travis asked, incredulous.

"You practise hockey, don't you?" Nish said as he hiked up his pants. "Why wouldn't you practise mooning?"

Buckling up his belt, Nish stepped away from the wet, snow-streaked window. Travis half ex-pected to see a line of police cars following them, lights flashing and sirens wailing. But there was only a van several hundred feet behind, its wipers beating furiously back and forth to fight the spray of the bus, the grey-haired driver staring straight ahead as if hypnotized by the road. He hadn't seen a thing.

But Travis had. He had seen his best friend, Mrs. Nishikawa's darling son, regular churchgoer and Boy Scout, *practising* mooning the entire world.

Travis had never experienced anything like New York City. The noise as they pulled off the turnpike ramp into the first streets of Manhattan was incredible, a city that hummed and howled in your ears. It seemed as if total panic had struck, as if around the next corner there must be a building on fire, a volcano erupting, or an invasion from outer space. Yellow taxis everywhere, everyone honking, pedestrians racing across streets as if they were being shot at rather than driven at. Police everywhere, too, laughing one minute and yelling the next as they directed the charging traffic. Vendors on every corner – roasted nuts, bagels, fresh fruit, newspapers, hot dogs, videos, books. And people, people, people. More people than Travis had ever seen.

Nish was first to discover that New York itself was a constant, moving Stupid Stop. The team was just checking into a small hotel on the corner of Lexington and East 52nd Street, about ten blocks from Times Square, when Nish wandered back from a nearby variety store with the first of his New York discoveries: a brand-new pair of sunglasses.

"They're Oakleys," he announced, naming one of the most expensive brands of wraparound glasses. "Five bucks," he added.

"Impossible," declared Sam. "You can't buy Oakleys for under a hundred."

"*I* can," Nish bragged. "And what about my watch?"

He held up his left arm and drew back the sleeve of his Screech Owls jacket with a dramatic flourish. A brand-new, heavy watch, hanging from Nish's wrist on a chunky gold wristband, flashed in the lobby lights.

Simon Milliken yanked Nish's wrist close and examined the watch like a jeweller. "It's a *Rolex*!" he gasped.

"Of course," agreed Nish. "Ten bucks."

"A Rolex costs two or three thousand!" Wilson shouted.

"Where'd you get 'em?" demanded Andy.

"Guy around the corner," Nish said. "He's got a whole briefcase full of them."

"Show me," said Andy. "I want to get a pair of sunglasses, too."

"So do I!" shouted Jesse.

"I want a Rolex!" said Simon.

Off they ran, with Nish leading the way — Oakley sunglasses perched high on his head, Rolex held out like he expected people to kiss his hand.

"That's stolen goods," said Derek. "They're going to get caught."

"They're not *real*," said Sarah. "They're knock-offs — phonies. They just look like the real thing. You wait: the logo on those sunglasses will rub off in a day and the watches won't be working by the time we leave."

"How do you know?" asked Fahd.

"My dad comes to New York all the time. He brought my mom back a fake Rolex and the hands fell off as she was putting it on. He thought it was a joke – she didn't think it was so funny, though."

"Aren't they illegal anyway?" asked Fahd.

"Of course. Illegal to sell, but not to buy. My dad says everybody buys them, either as souvenirs or to play a joke when they get back home."

Travis's curiosity was getting the better of him. He had resisted the urge to go along with the others, but now he worried that his team-mates might run into trouble or get lost.

Worrying was in Travis's nature. He put it down to having been lifelong buddies with Nish, who usually gave him a good reason to worry. Ever since he'd become team captain, Travis worried even more. He wanted everyone to get along. He wanted no trouble. Sometimes he thought if he ever stopped worrying, he would start worrying about *why* he was no longer worrying.

Travis slipped out the revolving door of the hotel. Nish had said he'd gone to the little store up Lexington and bought the watch and glasses just around the corner. Travis turned quickly and headed in that direction.

He couldn't see anyone, but then he clearly heard Nish's loud voice somewhere up ahead. He was bragging, showing off in front of his friends. He was talking about how much he could get for Oakley sunglasses and Rolex watches back home.

"I could *retire* at thirteen!" he shouted.

Travis turned a corner. His teammates were huddled into a narrow alleyway that ran between a dry cleaner's and the variety store. Andy was holding a shiny new watch, rolling it over and over in his palm. Simon was trying on a pair of sunglasses.

They had made their selections from a brown briefcase, the array of watches sparkling like buried treasure. The briefcase was being held open on the forearm of a very tall bearded man. He wore a long dark overcoat that reached almost to his feet. He had on brand-new Nike sneakers that looked as if they'd never before been tried on, let alone walked in. And he wore a strange, multicoloured hat pulled tight over his ears. Standing there in the shadows of the alley, he was hard to make out, apart from coat, shoes, hat, and beard – almost as if the clothes stood there empty, a clever dummy rigged to look like a very bad character.

The man peered out from below the brim of his odd hat, and Travis shivered as his icy gaze fell on him. The man then looked at Nish, who nodded as if to say Travis was all right.

Andy was fumbling in his wallet for money. The man held his hand out to take it.

Then, suddenly, without warning, he shoved the money back at Andy, grabbed the watch from him, and slammed the briefcase shut.

The boys jumped back, startled.

The man snarled once, turned, and began running farther down the alley.

"*I'll find you later!*" he called back over his shoulder.

"*Okay, Big!*" Nish shouted after him.

'Big'? Where did *that* come from, Travis wondered. Nish was already on a first-name basis?

Big?

"What happened?" Andy asked. He was staring into his empty palm, where moments ago the fake Rolex had glittered.

Nish said nothing, just nodded towards the opening of the alley onto Lexington Avenue.

A blue New York police car was idling on the street, a stocky policeman with dark glasses staring past them after the retreating Big.

Nish started cleaning his sunglasses on his shirt. He seemed so worldly all of a sudden. He was acting as if he'd lived and done business in New York all his life.

"Big don't like cops," Nish said, putting his sunglasses on again and heading out onto Lexington. He sounded like someone in a gangster movie.

More like "Cops don't like Big," Travis thought.

He didn't like Big either. He didn't like *any-thing* about this, not at all.

3

THEY HAD NO GAME AND NO PRACTICE THAT first day in New York City. Mr. Dillinger had arranged a terrific introduction to the Big Apple for them. They toured the city in a double-decker bus, stopping at the Empire State Building and then taking the ferry to the Statue of Liberty.

"What's wit' dis city and heights?" Nish asked the tour guide at the statue. "You wanna see me hurl, or what?"

Travis could hardly believe his ears. Ever since the back-alley meeting with the mysterious Big, Nish had been talking like he was the twelve-year-old head of the Mob.

They drove through Central Park and saw the outdoor rink where, Muck said, they might be holding one of their practices. Muck seemed genuinely excited by the prospect of getting out in the open air. Travis liked the idea, too. He could see skaters from the bus window, and none of them could skate very well. The Owls would be like an NHL team coming in to this little outdoor rink.

They journeyed through the theatre district and then, just off Times Square, Mr. Dillinger pointed out an old building called the Ed Sullivan Theatre where, he said, "The Late Show with David Letterman" was produced every night. Some of the Owls had seen the program, and they scrambled to the windows hoping to catch a glimpse of Letterman, the host. But all they could see were people walking fast with umbrellas held up to keep off the snow. No one in Tamarack ever used an umbrella against anything but rain. Travis thought it looked silly.

"I'm gonna be on dat show," New York Nish announced from the back of the bus.

The rest of the Owls turned to stare questioningly.

Fahd asked the obvious: "How?"

"I'll be famous – day after New Year's Eve."

"You won't be famous, "said Sam, "you'll be in jail!"

"This is the United States," Nish said, as if he was explaining something difficult to a child, "not Canada. In America, you get in the *Guinness Book of World Records*, you're an automatic star."

"Your *butt* will be the star, not you!" laughed Sarah.

"Laugh now – I'll be the one laughing later," Nish said with a sneer. "I've even worked out my own Top Ten list for when I'm on."

Most of them knew about Letterman's Top Ten list. Each school-day morning back in Tamarack, the local radio station played a tape of the previous night's list just before the eight o'clock news.

"What is it?" Fahd asked. Fahd always asked, even when others knew better than to play along with Nish's mad schemes.

"'The Top Ten Reasons Why Nish Should Be Captain,'" Nish announced.

Sarah's eyes went wide. As far as she or anyone else knew, Nish had never been considered for captain. Except, of course, by Nish.

Nish was in his glory, a deep red colour moving up into his face and making him all but glow as he began his countdown.

"Number ten," he began, "because he's won more most-valuable-player medals than anyone else on the Screech Owls."

Travis's first instinct was to try to figure out if that was so. He didn't think so. Surely it was Sarah.

Sam held up her hands to form a trumpet around her mouth and booed.

Everyone laughed.

"Number nine," Nish continued, "because he's got the best shot."

"*Boo!*" several Owls called at once.

"Number eight, because he's Muck's favourite."

"*Boooo!*" more Owls joined in.

"Number seven, because he's the fan favourite."

"*Booooooo!*"

"Number six, because he's the only Screech Owl who will ever make the NHL."

"*Boooooooo!*"

"Number five, because he's the best-looking of the Owls."

"*Boooooooo!*"

"Number four, because he's Paul Kariya's cousin!"

"*Boooooooooooo!*"

"Number three, because his equipment smells the best."

"*Boooooooooooo!*"

"Number two, because if he doesn't get it he's gonna hurl!"

"*Boooooooooooo!*"

"And number one," Nish announced, his eyes closed in private delight, "because he's the only peewee hockey player in the entire world listed in the *Guinness Book of World Records!*"

"BOOOOOOOOOOOOOOOOOOOOOO!!"

Travis had to cover his ears. The Owls were all booing and laughing at the same time. Nish was crimson, his natural colour whenever he was the centre of attention – which was almost always.

It was already an incredible trip.

4

IT HAD SNOWED ALL THROUGH THE NIGHT. Travis woke to the sound of the television blaring and Nish and Fahd battling over whether they watched "Simpsons" reruns (Nish's choice) or the New York City news (Fahd's choice). Fahd thought the traffic snarls were hilarious: the reporters and desk anchors were all talking about the snowfall in such worried voices that it seemed the city was being invaded.

In Tamarack, the snowploughs would have been out all night. The streets would be cleared, the roads sanded and salted. And every driver was as sure on snow in winter as they were on dry pavement in summer. A big snowfall was nothing.

But here the ploughs couldn't cope. Some broke down and others skidded off the road. The rest worked in vain to clear the roads for the more than a million commuters trying to get into the city. They had to close schools, cancel buses and trains, and all but shut down the city core. The snow was still falling, and the news-casters said city authorities were getting very worried, since there were only two days to go before New Year's Eve and the traditional Times Square celebrations.

Muck and Mr. Dillinger called an early-morning meeting in the lobby. The Owls stood around drinking orange juice and munching on doughnuts while Mr. Dillinger made some calls on his cellphone and then consulted with Muck.

"Our practice has been cancelled," Muck finally announced.

"The rink rats can't get to work," said Mr. Dillinger, shaking his head. "And the bus that was supposed to take us out isn't running."

The Owls groaned – but several of them, led by Nish, were faking their disappointment. Missing a practice, to Nish, was roughly equivalent to cancelling a dentist appointment.

"*Toooooooo baaaad*," Nish bawled, pretending to wipe tears from his eyes.

"The good news is, we got another one lined up," said Mr. Dillinger. "We're going to Central Park – the outside rink."

"YES!" shouted Sarah.

"ALL RIGHT!" yelled Sam, pumping her fist in the air.

It was fabulous news. The Owls loved nothing better than to skate on an outdoor rink. Ever since the day when all of Tamarack had frozen over and Muck Munro had joined his team for a game of shinny in the field, the Owls had begged for more chances to play on the hard natural ice of an outdoor rink. They'd loved the feel. They'd loved the way Muck had let them practise any silly thing they wanted. And they'd loved, most of all, the joyous look in Muck's face as he joined in, bad leg and all.

"Gather your equipment and be down here in five minutes," said Muck.

Muck wouldn't want it to show, but Travis was certain he detected the flicker of a smile on his old coach's face.

They walked to Central Park – a long line of peewee hockey players, each wearing a team jacket, equipment bags and sticks slung over their shoulders, leaning into the snow that was still falling hard along Lexington. They turned left at 59th Street, the buildings on the north side suddenly shielding them from the blowing snow, and they headed for the opening in the distance that signalled the beginning of the park.

They weren't alone. When the Owls arrived, there was already another team there. They had partially cleared off the ice, but the snow continued to build up fast. The team had fancy new jackets – "Burlington Bears" stitched across the back – and almost a half-dozen coaches were on the ice. The coach in charge – his jacket screamed "HEAD COACH" in capital letters – held a binder and clipboard and was setting out pylons all along one side.

He blew his whistle to call the team to attention. They gathered in the corner that offered the best shelter from the falling snow. As the Screech Owls filed by, Travis could see the head coach writing down a complicated drill on his clipboard. The ink was running in the melting snowflakes.

Travis laughed to himself, but he felt sorry for the team. He could see some faces through the masks and visors, and they didn't look particularly happy. The head coach seemed far more like a drill sergeant than anything.

Muck and Mr. Dillinger had the Owls dress quietly. There was a protected area where they could store their boots and jackets. Most of the Owls put their equipment on over their track suits for extra warmth, and some of them even squeezed their winter gloves into their hockey gloves for more insulation.

But not Nish. He kicked some snow out of the way, cleared off his seat, and dumped his equipment out at his feet, just as he would if they were back in the rink at home or in the fanciest dressing room in the National Hockey League.

"What's that *smell*?" Sarah asked.

"You have to ask?" Sam said. "It's Rolex Boy's equipment."

"Spread it around," Simon called. "It could melt the snow!"

"Very funny," Nish said, carefully removing his treasured fake Rolex and laying it on the bench.

"Watch still running?" Andy asked.

Nish didn't even check. "Of course it is. A Rolex has a lifetime guarantee."

"I suppose Mr. Big stands behind it," Sarah said.

"As a matter of fact, he does."

"What time is it, then?" Sam asked.

Nish wasn't about to get fooled. He checked the time on his watch. "You tell me," he said.

Sam made an elaborate show of checking her wristwatch: "Ten-fifteen."

Blood rushed to Nish's face. He checked his fake Rolex again, flashed a vicious look in Sam's direction, then practically pulled Fahd's arm out of its socket as he checked Fahd's wrist.

"Don't mess with me," Nish growled. "Nine-forty-six – same as I've got."

But no one was listening. The Owls were all laughing at the way Sam had tricked Nish into thinking his fancy new Rolex had already gone bad. He finished dressing in silence, periodically flashing a stare of pure evil in Sam's direction.

The team on the ice was still going through drills when the Screech Owls came out.

The head coach looked up, shrugged in what appeared to be disappointment, then blew hard on his whistle. All the Bears stopped instantly. He skated over to Muck.

They seemed such a contrast: the Bears' coach with the "HEAD COACH" lettering on his new jacket, his team track suit, team cap, big shiny whistle around his neck, clipboard under his arm; Muck in his ragged old sweats, his old junior jacket badly faded, his old hockey gloves and stick. No clipboard. Not even a whistle.

"You Muck Munro from Canada?" the head coach asked.

Muck nodded.

"Head coach Rod Peters from Burlington, Vermont. I understand we're to share this facility today."

"So they tell me," said Muck.

"I've already run my gang through some basic drills. You can either join in or we can split up – or, if you want, you can run some drills of your own."

"I wouldn't mind," said Muck.

The head coach seemed to be looking for a binder under Muck's arm. But there was none there.

"You want to borrow some of our pylons?" the head coach asked.

Muck shook his head.

"I have some U.S. hockey drills here – you want to borrow one or two?" the head coach said, pushing his clipboard towards Muck.

Muck shook his head.

"You got everything you need, then?" the head coach asked.

Muck held up the puck he was holding. "Everything," he said.

"Well," the head coach said impatiently, "what's the drill, then?"

Muck smiled at him. "You go sit over there. Five on at a time. Six, counting goalies. No whistles. One hour of good old shinny."

The head coach looked at Muck as if he had just walked out of a past century. "*Shinny?*" he said, as if it were a swear word. "You want these kids to play *shinny?*"

"Not just them," Muck said. "I plan to play, too. You're welcome to join in if you like."

"YESSS!" shouted Sarah.

"YAAY, MUCK!" shouted Sam, pounding her stick on the ice.

The head coach looked dumbfounded. He could not believe what Muck was proposing. Nor could he believe the reaction of the Screech Owls. Nor could he cope with his own team, who began shouting and pounding their sticks on the ice the same as the Owls. Disgusted, he skated away, calling his several assistants over to join him.

Muck held the first faceoff – and that was it: from that point on, no whistles or faceoffs or coaching. He skated off to wait his own turn, and as soon as Nish took his first break Muck stepped into the lineup himself at defence.

Travis couldn't have been happier. He loved the way his skates cut into natural ice, almost as if he were shaping it rather than simply sliding over it. He loved the raspy sound his blades made in the hard ice and the way the chips flew when he came to a quick stop.

Sarah was in her element, too. She was the best skater on the Owls, and by far the best skater on the outdoor rink. There were a few people walking through the park, a few even on cross-country skis, and when they stopped to watch the game, Travis knew it was Sarah who had caught their eye. Not just because she was a girl – the Owls had several girl players, and the Bears had a couple as well – but because of the extraordinary grace she showed moving up and down the ice, whether she had the puck or not.

Nish had realized almost instantly that the Owls had far more talent than the Bears, and so he began showing off. He tried to skate through the Bears backwards carrying the puck, and almost scored on a backhand as he slipped by their net, howling like a wolf.

Travis felt a tap on his shin.

It was Muck, sweat pouring off his face, snow melting in his hair. "You, me 'n' Sarah," he said. "We're switching sides."

Travis watched in amazement as Muck went over and talked to the one Bears assistant coach who'd come out to play. The head coach was still standing back, shaking his head as if some crime had been committed by the Owls and their stubborn coach. Muck switched jackets with the assistant coach, and Travis and Sarah switched sweaters with two of the weaker Bears players.

Muck rapped his stick on the ice. "Now we got us a game."

Travis's heart almost jumped through his jersey. It was no big deal, a game of shinny on an outdoor rink, but it felt as if he was playing in Madison Square Garden. He could see that more and more people were stopping to watch. He supposed with so many offices and businesses closed for the storm, there were a lot of people around with nothing to do. They'd gone out for a walk in the snow, and ended up at a hockey game.

It was wonderful playing with Muck. He couldn't skate all that well with his bad leg, but his passes were what the Owls called "NHL passes," so hard they almost snapped the stick out of your hand. And always, always on the tape.

The people who had gathered to watch were starting to cheer the better plays. And a television crew had appeared, the cameraman hurrying to get shots from ice level, and then of the small crowd that had formed to watch this pick-up hockey game in the heart of Central Park.

Muck sent Travis up left wing, and Travis danced around the one defenceman, leaving just

Nish backing up between Travis and Sarah and the Owls' goal. Travis cut one way and Sarah cut the other way, the two of them criss-crossing right in front of Nish. Travis faked a drop pass to Sarah, but Nish was too smart and wouldn't go for it.

Travis held, and looked back over his shoulder. Muck was charging up ice, moving as fast as his bad leg would permit. He was rapping the ice hard for a pass.

Travis zipped it back to Muck.

Nish read the play perfectly, and dove to cut off Muck.

Then Muck did something astonishing. He flicked the puck so it flew just over Nish's sprawling body and then leaped off his good leg and took flight himself, right over the spinning defenceman.

Muck and the puck landed in the clear. Travis could hear Muck laughing and whooping. Muck faked a pass to Travis, backhanded one to Sarah, and Sarah ripped the puck high into the net behind Jeremy.

The three of them – Muck, Sarah, and Travis – crashed together into the corner and fell into the soft snow that had built up along the boards. They were all laughing. Their new teammates from the Bears also ploughed in on them, everyone tapping their shins and patting them on the back of their pants.

The television cameraman was right in there with them. Travis looked back. No, there were two cameras now. *No, make that three!*

Sarah skated back, passing Nish, still sprawled on the ice, hands and legs out, red face beaming as he licked the melting snow that fell through his mask and onto his hot face.

"Get the time of that goal, Rolex Boy?" Sarah asked as she passed.

"Very funny," Nish snorted. But he was laughing. One of the cameramen moved in tight to Nish, and Nish obliged by flicking his chin strap and sending his helmet flying along the ice.

Everyone was laughing.

Even the head coach was smiling. He, too, was coming out to join in the game. He seemed a bit sheepish at first, but there was no doubt he wanted to play.

Perhaps he'd never known that hockey could be such fun.

5

"THAT'S ME! IT'S ME! ME! ME!"

Nish was screaming and pointing, though there was no need for either. They were in their hotel room – Travis, Nish, Andy, Simon, Jesse, and Derek – and no one had trouble recognizing their friend. Of course it was him: *who else?* Nish, flat on his back, his helmet rolling along the ice, snow falling and melting over his hot, beet-red face.

The neat thing was, this was NBC Television, the nightly New York City newscast, and after nearly twenty minutes of traffic accidents and closed schools, the anchor had turned to a "lighter side of the storm." Suddenly there were shots of people cross-country skiing in Central Park and of the great shinny game between the Burlington Bears of Vermont and the Screech Owls from some small town in far-off Canada.

"It's Tamarack, idiot," Jesse shouted at the screen. "Tamarack! And we don't live in igloos, and we don't eat snow, and we weren't all born with skates on!"

"Speak for yourself," Nish said. "I could skate before I was toilet-trained."

Andy held his nose. "And when did you get toilet-trained? We must have missed it."

They were all laughing when there was a knock at the door. Andy jumped up, peeped out the spy glass, and announced, "Fahd."

"Let him in," said Derek.

"See me on da news?" Nish called to Fahd in his stupid New York accent.

Fahd shook his head. He looked excited.

"We've got something far more interesting to see," he announced.

"*What?*" several of the boys asked at once.

"You want to talk to Lars?" Fahd asked.

"He's *here*?" said Simon.

"Kind of – come on!"

The room Fahd was sharing with Data was on a lower floor, and everything was spaced out a little more to allow easy passage for Data's wheelchair. There was even a closet with the shelves and rails set low so that Data could arrange his clothes without having to stand. No closet, of course, was ever as low as Nish's; his closet was the floor, where he dumped all the clothes he'd need at the start of every tournament.

Data and Fahd had been busy. Fahd had brought along his father's digital video camera, which was now connected to Data's new lap-top, which in turn was connected to the phone. Somehow, Fahd and Data had figured out how to hook up to the Internet, dial free of charge to Sweden, and connect with Lars, who had a similar setup at his uncle's place in Stockholm.

Data was on-line with Lars as they came in. Fahd's camera was set up to take in the room, and as they entered, they saw Lars on Data's computer screen. He was smiling and waving.

"Hey, guys!" a disembodied voice said from the computer. It sounded a little tinny, a bit hollow, a bit scratchy – but it was Lars's voice, no doubt. "Yo! Nish!" the voice crackled over the computer. "How's it going? You moon the world yet?"

"I'm working on it," Nish said. He looked slightly confused, almost as if he suspected this was some sort of weird trick Fahd and Data were pulling on him.

"Hi, Trav," Lars said, waving.

Travis waved back, uncertainly. Lars seemed both there and *not* there. His movements weren't as fluid as they would be on a video. It was as if a new picture of Lars was being received every microsecond, which, Travis figured, is probably precisely how it worked.

"Hey, Lars!" Travis called back. "You playing any hockey?"

"I'm in a tournament," Lars's voice crackled back. "Same as you guys. It's with my old team. I can hardly remember how to play the game the way it's played over here," he laughed.

"Simple," said Nish. "Never shoot, pass backwards, take a dive whenever anyone comes near you."

"*Thank you, Don Cherry!*" Lars shouted, sending Nish a raspberry across seven time zones.

They talked a while longer. Data used the mouse to control the camera, zooming in and out and focusing on whichever Owl happened to be talking to Lars.

Nish took very little part in the conversation. He seemed too interested in how the whole video-telephone call was happening. Travis had never before seen his friend so keenly interested in anything to do with computers. If it was a computer game, in which Nish could destroy the world with bombs and flame-throwers, then he was interested. But never before in how a computer actually worked.

Nish came back to life after they'd all said goodbye to Lars and promised to check in on him each day. They'd tell him how they were doing in the Big Apple tournament; he'd bring them up to date in how the peewee tournament in Stockholm was going.

But Nish had other ideas. "How's this work?"

Data explained. He talked about Internet long-distance calls and video transmission and how the cameras sent images so quickly it was almost as good as television reception.

"Television, eh?" Nish said.

Travis had seen that look before. He half expected to hear Nish's little brain shift gears, grinding and whining like a truck attempting to break free of a snowbank.

"Tell me, Data," Nish began, "when they broadcast the New Year's Eve countdown, how do they do that?"

"It's live television," Data said. "It's simple. They have cameras on the guy doing the count-down and project it onto the big screen. They'll have a temporary studio set up at Times Square."

"As simple as this?" Nish asked, nodding at Data's laptop.

"No. But not much more complicated."

"Can you 'bump' a broadcast?"

"I don't follow," Data said, turning his chair around to stare at Nish. He clearly had no idea where Nish was going with this. Unlike Travis, who was cringing at the thought.

"You know, can you cut in? Could you run your own broadcast and bump the one they're showing?"

Data thought about it a moment. "I suppose so. There'd be two or three cameras and a direc-tor controlling the shots. You'd have to break into their feed."

Nish sat, silently working his mouth.

If a brain could chew gum, his was blowing bubbles.

6

TRAVIS UNDERSTOOD HIS CRAZY FRIEND'S SCHEME
instantly. It hadn't taken Nish long to put the
camera and the computer together in his imagination and end up with his own big bare butt
staring into the faces of a billion New Year's Eve
celebrants.

"Don't even think about it," Travis warned his
friend.

"Too late," Nish advised.

It was always "too late" with Nish. Travis was
well used to that by now.

Fahd and Data, unfortunately, were intrigued.
They hadn't any burning desire to see Nish's bare
butt exposed for the entire world to enjoy, but
they were computer nuts and endlessly fascinated
by how things worked. Nish had posed a puzzle,
and they just couldn't resist the challenge.

"Frighteningly simple," said Data after he
and Fahd had consulted. "Production feeds are
done by telephone lines. If you could call into
the studio somehow, all you'd have to do is
override their broadcast with yours. You'd need
numbers and passwords, but if you had that you

could bump them for a bit. I don't know how long, though."

"*Long enough for my butt!*" Nish shouted triumphantly.

"You'll get caught," Travis warned. He couldn't help himself. He was captain, after all. He was responsible.

Nish shot him a withering look. He looked as if Travis had just suggested he might get in trouble for talking in class – which, for Nish, was pretty much a daily ritual back in Tamarack.

"If the world was filled with people like you," Nish sneered, "there'd be no *Guinness Book of World Records.*"

Travis said nothing, but he couldn't help thinking, If the world was filled with people like you, Nish, there'd be no world!

The snow continued to fall. One of the weather reporters called it "The Storm of the Century," which made the Screech Owls chuckle. If this was the worst storm New York City had ever seen, they ought to come to Tamarack for a week in January. Back home, every storm was "The Storm of the Century" by New York standards.

Still, it was coming down hard. The streets were filled with snow. The ploughs couldn't cope, and even when they did get down one of the jam-packed New York streets, they seemed to be ploughing the wrong way, pushing huge mounds of snow into the centre instead of to the side. They had front-end loaders out to fill the snow trucks, but the snow trucks kept getting stuck, which only made matters worse.

The mayor declared a city emergency. The governor declared a state emergency. About the only thing that remained was for the president of the United States to declare war on the storm. What would he do? wondered Travis. Blast the cloud cover off with a missile?

Mr. Dillinger organized a walk to check out the huge Christmas tree at Rockefeller Center. Everyone came along, even Muck. They threw snowballs and sang Christmas carols as they strolled.

It was, in its own way, an extraordinarily beautiful day: the snow falling in huge, damp clumps, the streets white and glowing with Christmas lights, the people wandering about as if they'd never seen anything like it. The Big Apple was turning into the Big Marshmallow.

At Rockefeller Center a crew was struggling to keep the small ice surface clear, but it was almost impossible. There were a few skaters, and they left trails behind them in the snow.

The Owls were standing around the huge, twinkling Christmas tree when suddenly a familiar sound ripped through the silence of the falling snow.

"KA–WA–BUN–GA!"

Travis and Sarah raced over to the railings to stare down onto the rink, which was well below street level.

It was Nish! He had rented a pair of odd-looking, black-booted skates and was heading out onto the ice all by himself.

Only he wasn't skating, he was sailing – swooping about in the exaggerated style of a figure skater. He turned quickly backwards and, with his arms still flying dance-style, picked up speed as he rounded the rink. Suddenly he stabbed one toe down and leaped into the air in a ridiculous attempt at a Salchow – only to slip and land flat on his rear end, spinning across the ice.

The Owls, now all gathered around the railings, howled with laughter.

Travis noticed a television crew over by the Christmas tree. They were gathering up their equipment and racing towards the rink.

"KA–WA–BUN–GA!"

Same call, different voice. It was *Sam* – same rented skates, same silly exaggerated drift out onto the ice. She skated over to where Nish lay and stopped suddenly, deliberately shooting snow into his face.

Nish laughed. He got up, bowed deeply, and held out his arms.

"*What are they doing?*" Sarah shouted, laughing.

Sam bowed in return, like an old-fashioned lady accepting a dance, and then, with her nose stuck high in the air, she linked arms with Nish and the two of them began skating around in perfect rhythm, noses aloft, eyes practically shut, each kick long and exaggerated.

If Travis didn't know better, he'd swear he was watching the dance competition at the Olympics.

The people standing around began to clap and cheer. The Owls were shouting down — KA-WA-BUN-GA!" called Fahd in a voice that didn't seem to fit — and Muck and Mr. Dillinger were leaning over the railing, laughing. Mr. Dillinger was wiping away tears.

The camera moved in tight, following the two Olympic "ice-dancers" until, on one corner, Sam decided to turn the tables on poor Nish and lift him over her head.

Sam was strong. There wasn't a member of the team who didn't marvel at her strength, but Nish was still Nish. Sam grunted and tried to hoist him high. For a moment Travis's imagination got the better of him and he could see Sam skating triumphantly about the ice surface, one hand waving free while the other held Nish high in the air, her partner's arms swaying to the music and a rose between his teeth.

Sadly, the truth was not so elegant. Sam tried, and Nish lost his balance. For a second he left the ice — screamed, "I'M GONNA HURL!" — and then, with the crowd gasping, the two of them crashed in a pile and flew into the corner. They lay on their backs, laughing and letting the snow fall into their open mouths.

The camera caught it all.

The Screech Owls raced down the wide steps, turned onto the ice surface, and ran, sliding, across to the fallen Olympic heroes.

Nish blinked up towards the camera zooming in on him. "Which newscast?" he asked, as if being filmed had become a daily experience for him.

The cameraman continued to shoot. A woman – the producer? – leaned over from behind the camera and smiled.

"Not news," she said. "'Letterman.'"

Nish's eyes went wide. "'Letterman?'"

"'The Late Show,'" she said. "You know."

"This is for 'Letterman'?" Nish said.

"We're just doing shots of the storm," she said. "This was great. Thanks a lot."

"When?" Nish asked.

"Tonight," the woman said.

Nish closed his eyes, huge flakes falling onto his face and melting instantly on his hot, sweating flesh. He looked as if he had died and gone to heaven.

"I'm gonna be on 'Letterman,'" he kept saying to himself. "*I'm gonna be on 'Letterman'!*"

7

NISH WALKED BACK TOWARDS THE HOTEL AS IF the air was filled with falling ticker tape, not snow. Travis had rarely seen his puffed-up pal so full of himself.

"I'm gonna be on 'Letterman'! I'm gonna be on 'Letterman'!"

Not *we're* going to be on 'Letterman'! Not *Sam and I* are going to be on 'Letterman'! *I'm* gonna be on 'Letterman'! If I hear that one more time, thought Travis, I'm – I'm gonna hurl!

They passed Lexington on their way to the little hotel. They were tired, and Mr. Dillinger and Muck had suggested they get back and rest up for the evening game. The two men saw them back to within sight of the hotel and then turned in the other direction. Muck wanted to see the New York Public Library, which might have struck the Owls as a bit odd if it had been anyone but Muck. But they knew him only too well; he'd rather read a book than go to a movie, rather visit an old Civil War battleground than go to DisneyWorld.

Nish and Travis and several of the boys were lagging behind the rest when a strange sound cut through the falling snow.

"*Psssssst!*"

Travis wasn't sure it was a voice at first. But then it came again, sharp and fast: "*Psssst – Nish!*"

They were just passing by a small alley, so narrow a car couldn't get through. There was a large, dark figure looming there, covered from head to toe in heavy winter clothing.

It was Big!

"*Yo! Big!*" shouted Nish as if he'd just bumped into a long-lost friend. "*Whazzup?*"

The New York accent was back.

Big waved them into the shadowed alleyway. "You still want them watches 'n' things?" he asked.

"Sure do, man," said Nish. "Right, boys?"

Andy, Fahd, and Wilson all agreed. They pressed closer as Big opened up his "treasure chest."

Travis couldn't help himself. It seemed as if the watches and sunglasses had a magnetic quality. They were *pulling* him into the alleyway.

This time there were no police passing by. Travis supposed they were all tied up with traffic problems. Big didn't seem at all worried as he showed his fake Rolexes and sunglasses.

Andy, Wilson, Fahd, Jesse, and Derek all bought stuff. Even Travis found his hand reaching for his wallet as he rolled a fancy-looking Swiss Army watch around in the palm of his hand.

"I'm gonna be on 'Letterman,'" Nish told Big.

Big blinked. He clearly didn't believe it. A man who dealt in fooling people wasn't going to be easily fooled himself. "How so, man?"

Nish grinned from ear to ear. "They filmed me skating up at Rockefeller Center."

"True?"

"True – and I'll be on again, too, right after I moon 'em all New Year's Eve."

Big, who'd been taking money from the other boys, turned with a perplexed look on his face. "You what?"

"We got a plan," Nish went on. "Fahd here, and Data, he's back at the hotel, they got it all figured out how we can bump the live broadcast and get my bare butt on the big TV screen over on Times Square."

Travis wished Nish would just shut up. This was a stupid thing to imagine, let alone tell a total stranger.

But Big was interested. For the first time, he smiled, flashing a gold tooth. Travis did a double take. He hadn't seen a gold tooth since Sweden, when the Russian mob had kidnapped him and several other peewee hockey players.

He wondered for a moment if Big's gold tooth was a knock-off, too – maybe made of plastic and painted gold.

"Tell me more," said Big.

"Fahd and Data are computer geniuses," said Nish. "We got a video camera and we got a system all figured out where we can bump off the regular programming and get me on for a minute – it's gonna get me in da *Guinness Book of World Records*, Big."

"I'm sure it will," said Big. "If it doesn't get you busted."

"Not a chance," said Nish. "We got it all figured out – they won't even know what happened until it's too late."

Travis couldn't help himself. He poked Nish in the ribs. Nish turned slightly and swatted at Travis as if he were a pesky mosquito.

The boys had all the fake watches and sunglasses they could afford. Big rolled up his loot and closed the half-empty briefcase. Travis wondered how much of a killing he'd made. What were the ten-dollar watches really worth? Five? Two?

"See you around, eh, Big?" Nish said as they departed.

"You bet, Nish," said Big with another flash of his gold tooth. "I'll watch for you on 'Letterman.'"

8

THE SCREECH OWLS PLAYED THEIR FIRST GAME IN the Big Apple International Peewee Tournament that evening. It was, for the Owls, little more than a warm-up. The team they were up against, the Long Island Selects, weren't much better than the Burlington Bears. The main difference was that this game would count in the standings; the shinny game against the Bears mattered only as a memory.

Sam and Sarah both played exceptional games. Sam was back on defence, and she blocked shots and carried the puck and helped Jeremy clear away rebounds so easily it seemed she might keep the Selects off the scoreboard all on her own.

Sarah was in one of her playmaking moods. It didn't matter how many times Travis or Dmitri set her up, she would pass the puck off. She simply refused to take an easy shot on goal, dropping the puck back to the point instead, or spinning around to try to set up Dmitri or Travis. By the third period, Dmitri and Travis had two goals each, and Nish also had two pinching in from the point.

"Slow it down," Muck instructed during a brief break.

He didn't need to say any more. Every one of the Screech Owls knew how Muck refused to embarrass another team or coach in a tournament. Even in a tournament where it was possible the standings might be decided by the number of goals scored, Muck would refuse to let the Owls run up the score.

An instruction of no more scoring was like an invitation to Nish. If a game truly mattered, if the Owls absolutely *had* to have a goal, there was no one they'd want on the ice more than Nish. Nish, even more than Sarah, had the knack of scoring when it counted. But take away a reason to get serious, and Nish would try anything, no matter how crazy. His big ambition, he'd told Travis, was to score a "Pavel Bure goal": taking the puck behind the opposition cage, flipping it high into the air so it floated back over the goal, and then skating out in front quickly enough to be there in time to baseball the puck into the net. He must have tried it a hundred times in practice, without a single success.

But Nish was nothing if not determined. He picked up the puck behind his own net, skated out slowly, and faked a pass up to Liz on the left, then broke with the puck into the open space.

Travis was sitting on the bench when Nish began his charge. He lowered his head, almost wishing he weren't in the same building.

"The show's on," said Sarah, sitting beside him.

"I know," said Travis.

And what a show it was. Nish skated up and cut diagonally across centre, stickhandling beautifully. He had his head up, and Travis wondered if it was to see if there were any cameras on him.

Nish worked his way across the Selects' blueline and down into the corner. He then faked a pass to Sam, who was charging in from the far point. Sam angrily slammed her stick onto the ice when Nish hung on. He had other ideas. He kept stickhandling behind the net, watching.

"Here comes his 'Bure,'" Travis announced on the bench.

"Such a surprise!" said Sarah.

Nish tapped the puck so it stood on edge, then lifted it high so it floated, spinning, over the net and over the head of the little Long Island goaltender.

Nish dug in hard, churning round to the front. He flew out from the boards and passed the left post moving backwards, away from the net, the puck still in the air.

He swung mightily, the play perfect – except for one small detail. He missed the puck, and fell with the effort.

A huge laugh went up from the sparse crowd watching in this little rink down by the East River.

Nish got up and chased hard back down the ice as the Selects managed a three-on-one break and scored on a good screen shot that ripped into Jeremy's glove and then trickled into the Owls' net.

"He's benched," Sarah said, as she shifted over to make room for the players coming off.

"Guaranteed," agreed Travis.

Nish came off, his face beet red, and didn't even bother looking over at Muck. What was the point? He plopped down beside Travis, ripped his helmet off, picked up the water bottle, and sprayed his face, hair and, a bit, into his open mouth. He swallowed, spat, and turned to Travis.

"What's with Muck?" he asked.

"You have to ask?" Travis said.

"I'm benched," Nish said as if it were an announcement.

"You're surprised?"

"Hey," Nish grinned. "He told us not to score, didn't he? What more can I do for this team?"

Travis grabbed the water bottle and sprayed it as hard as he could directly into his own face.

It did no good. When he opened his eyes Nish was still sitting there, smiling at him.

"*It's time!*" called Fahd, as if they didn't know.

It was also way past bedtime. Mr. Dillinger had said there was a 10:30 curfew — "Lights out and no portable CD players!" It was now

11:30, and while the lights were out, no one was asleep. The television was on, flickering like a ghost at the foot of the beds where six of the Owls lay, watching and waiting.

"Think they'll open with me?" Nish asked no one in particular.

The "Late Show" was just coming on. Letterman was doing his stand-up act, an endless string of jokes about the storm, half of which the Owls didn't get, and then came an interview with a giggling, gum-chewing actress about being stranded in a taxi and missing her opening-night act at one of the New York theatres.

"*Bor-ring!*" Nish moaned.

"We've got some footage from around the city," Letterman said to the still-giggling actress. "Would you like to see what the storm did to a few other New Yorkers?"

"Yeah, sure," she said, snapping her gum.

"Here we go," announced Fahd.

With David Letterman cracking more jokes in the background, they showed dozens of clips of the city coping with the Storm of the Century.

There was a rhinoceros at the zoo pawing the snow like he'd never seen it before. Letterman cracked a joke about Africa.

There was a beggar lying on the street, cup held out and brimming with snow. Letterman cracked a joke about being poor that Travis didn't like.

There were shots of cross-country skiers in Central Park, a dozen shots of people trying to push or pull their cars free of snowdrifts, several shots of people falling on the street – all accompanied by more cracks by Letterman.

But nothing about Rockefeller Center. Nothing about the outdoor skating rink.

Nothing about the two "Olympic ice-dancers."

Nothing about Nish.

"*What kind of rip-off is this?*" Nish howled when the footage stopped and the show returned to the host and his guest, now with a full-blown bubble hiding her face.

"Maybe they're saving you?" Fahd suggested.

Nish liked the suggestion. "Yeah, they're saving the best for last," he said.

But there was nothing more. Travis grew sleepy, turned around, and tucked himself into his bed. He heard Fahd do the same, and eventually the television was clicked off and the odd colours stopped dancing around the room. It was pitch black, and very, very late.

It grew quiet, very quiet, and then Travis heard Nish clear his throat.

"It means I *have* to moon now," Nish said.

No one said anything back to him.

"I've *no* choice."

9

"WE LOST."

Lars's voice was shaky coming over the line. But whether it was the transmission or Lars himself, Travis couldn't tell. Lars always took losses hard. There was no reason why he wouldn't take a loss with his old team in Sweden just as badly.

"We won – easily!" Nish practically shouted into the small microphone Fahd had set up so they could all speak more easily to Lars.

They talked for about fifteen minutes. Lars was finding it difficult readjusting to European-style hockey. He partly blamed himself for losing the game. They talked a bit more about every-thing the Owls had been doing in New York and then Lars signed off. He had a game to go to.

"Fahd and I have been thinking about this," Data said as he turned off his laptop. He turned towards Nish. "And I e-mailed a couple of com-puter buddies back in Canada. There's no way you can do that thing you want to do live."

"I can't?" said Nish, suddenly distraught.

"We'll film it on this camera and save it on the computer," Data explained. "That way, if we can actually jump into the transmission, all I'll need to do is click the mouse a couple of times."

"And you won't have to freeze your butt off," added Fahd.

"*But it's not the same!*" Nish whined.

"What do you mean?" asked Data. "It'll still be your butt up there – no one else's – so what's it matter if you do it live or not?"

"But it's no good," Nish protested. "It's like – like the difference between a goal and an assist."

Travis couldn't believe his ears. Only Nish would think of something like that. Travis prided himself on his assists. And Sarah had once said she'd rather set up a pretty goal than score one herself.

"Take it or leave it," said Data. "It's the only way."

Nish was wringing his hands. His expression kept twisting back and forth between agony and disappointed acceptance.

Finally he said, "Okay – when do we do it?"

"Right now's as good a time as any," said Fahd.

Nish looked up in surprise. "*Here?*" he asked.

"Sure," said Fahd. "Why not? We have the camera out anyway. Data can then save it to disk."

"*Here?*" Nish practically wailed.

Data shook his head. "Here is where we are, Nish. Let's get it done."

Nish looked around the room, panicking. "Not with all *you* here!"

"What's your problem?" asked Andy.

"No way I'm mooning any camera unless you guys leave," Nish announced. "Fahd and Data can stay."

Travis couldn't help himself. He leaped up off the bed to face his best friend. "Let me get this straight," he said. "You want to moon Times Square and a billion people around the world – but no way you're dropping your pants in front of your own friends."

"*No!*" Nish almost shouted. "I need privacy."

Travis started walking towards the door. "You need a psychiatrist," he said.

Nish, looking miserable, shot out his tongue in response.

"We're outta here," Travis announced, pulling the door open. The rest of the Owls, the three plotters excluded, were right behind him.

"We'll leave you here to make an ass of yourself," Travis said.

"Very funny," Nish snarled. "Very, very funny."

They played again that afternoon. They were lucky. The continuing storm made it impossible to reach the outlying rinks in Rye and Long Island, and so more of the games had to be scheduled as close to downtown as possible.

"We've had a change of facilities," Mr. Dillinger announced at lunch.

"What rinky-dink rink are we at next?" Nish asked. He hadn't been impressed with the facility for their game against the Selects. "Or are we playing this one outdoors?"

"Not quite," said Mr. Dillinger, no longer able to hide his smile. "This one's at Madison Square Garden."

"*MSG!*" Fahd shouted.

"The one and only," said Mr. Dillinger. "Let's get going."

All Travis's worries were suddenly lifted from his shoulders. He no longer cared about the storm. He no longer even thought about Nish and his ridiculous scheme to get himself – or at least a *part* of himself – into the *Guinness Book of World Records*. All he could think about was that he was going to play at the rink where Wayne Gretzky had played his very last game.

It was a rink like no other he had ever seen. They entered at a huge side entrance, big enough to take a tractor trailer and a bus, and then walked up a long spiral ramp that left them breathless. "The ice surface is six floors up," said Mr. Dillinger.

They came out at the Zamboni entrance and then turned left into the narrow corridor leading to the dressing rooms. They would be dressing in the visitors' room, where Orr and Dryden and Paul Kariya had dressed.

After he had his shin pads and pants on, Travis went out and walked up and down the corridor in his socks. All along the walls were huge, photographs of famous people who had played Madison Square Garden. He walked along, checking the names: Elton John, Frank Sinatra, Judy Garland, the Beatles, Wayne Nishikawa . . .

Wayne Nishikawa?

Travis stopped so abruptly he slipped in his socks and almost fell.

Nish?

Taped over the photograph, with black hockey tape, was one of Nish's hockey cards from the Quebec Peewee tournament. Nish's smiling mug was covering the face of Elvis Presley. Nish's name – cut, it seemed, from the program for the Big Apple tournament – had also been taped over Elvis Presley's name at the bottom of the framed picture. Nish's mother would have been outraged. She called Elvis Presley "The King" and had most of his records.

"Like it?" a voice called from down the corridor.

It was Nish, half-dressed, sticking his head out the dressing-room door. He was grinning.

"I'm sure Elvis would be pleased," said Travis.

"He's dead," Nish said. "I'm the new King."

"King of *what?*" Travis asked.

"King of Hockey," Nish began. "King a da Big Apple. King of the *Guinness Book of World Records* – you name it."

Okay, Travis thought, I will. He forced a grin back at his weird friend: "King of Jerks."

Nish suddenly looked hurt. "What's dat for?" he asked.

"You're acting stupid," Travis said. "You're going way overboard on everything. That stupid New York talk. That stupid mooning idea that's just going to get everybody in trouble."

"Relax," Nish said, his old grin rising back into his face. "Nobody's gonna get hurt."

"They better not," said Travis.

Nish shook his head. "Relax, pal. Enjoy the Big Apple. And don't forget – one day you'll be able to say you knew me."

"What good's that, even if you do it? It's not like anybody's going to know it's you."

"My *butt* will be world-famous," Nish said. "It'll be like saying you saw Niagara Falls being formed, or the pyramids being built – you know what I mean?"

Travis just shook his head. No, he didn't know what Nish meant. And when he tried to force his mind to work it through, it was like his brain was a computer that had suddenly crashed.

10

THEY WERE TO PLAY A TEAM FROM MICHIGAN
called the Detroit Wheels, one of the top-ranked
peewee teams in the United States.

Muck seemed apprehensive. "This is a smart
team," he said. "Well coached and well condi-
tioned. You make a mistake, it's in our net. So we
play safe at all times – *understand, Nishikawa?*"

"Understand, Coach," Nish mumbled, his
head between his shin pads, his helmet on, his
stare straight down between his legs.

Sarah rolled her eyes at Travis from across
the dressing room. They both knew how much
Muck hated being called "Coach" – "This isn't
football," he'd say, "I'm 'Muck' or, if you have to,
'Mr. Munro,' but I am *not* 'Coach' " – but they also
knew that Nish was in game mode, head down,
full concentration. Travis took it as a good sign.

Travis had played in a lot of wonderful rinks:
the Olympic rink in Lake Placid where the
Miracle On Ice game had been won, the Quebec
Colisée during the Quebec Peewee, Maple Leaf
Gardens in Toronto before they built the Air
Canada Centre, the Globen Rink in Stockholm,

and even Big Hat Arena in Nagano, Japan. But still Madison Square Garden was special. It was as if they were skating under a huge, sprawling, golden church ceiling. And the seats somehow seemed closer to the ice, even though that was impossible. The Stanley Cup banners and retired jerseys in the rafters only made it feel all the more important, all the more special.

Travis liked the feeling of being here. He liked the way Nish had prepared for the game. He liked the way Sarah had skated during warm-up, her strides so smooth it sounded like she was cutting paper with scissors as she took the corners. He liked the fact that he hit the crossbar with his first shot of the warm-up.

The Wheels were bigger than the Owls. They were bigger and stronger and played a more physical game. First shift out, Nish got hammered into a corner on a play that Mr. Dillinger shouted should have been a penalty. No penalty was called, and Nish got right back up and into the game. No grandstanding.

"We're faster," Muck said after the first few shifts. "We can get a step on them. Speed is still the most intimidating thing in hockey – don't forget that when you're out there."

Travis felt Muck was speaking directly to him. To him and to Simon and to Jesse and to Fahd and to Liz – the smallest Owls, the ones most likely to be frightened away from the corners by the huge all-male Wheels. It felt to Travis as if they were playing against *men*, not other twelve-year-olds.

"Check out number 6," Sarah said after she and Dmitri and Travis came off from a shift. "He's got a moustache."

Travis tried to see through the other player's mask. It was difficult to say for sure, but it certainly looked like the beginnings of a moustache. He shuddered. Perhaps they *were* men. Perhaps there had been a mistake in the scheduling.

The Wheels scored first, and second, both times by essentially running over the smaller members of the Owls. Once Fahd coughed up the puck. The other time Wilson dropped it for Simon, who was simply bowled over by a larger Detroit player.

Muck showed no nervousness at all. "Use your speed," he said to Sarah at one point, laying a big hand on her shoulder for support.

Next shift, Nish made a wonderful block on a good Wheels opportunity and jumped up and moved the puck behind his own net. He fed it up along the boards to Travis, who used his skates to tick it out onto his stick blade. A large Wheels defenceman was pinching in hard on him.

Travis's original plan was to dump it out through centre and trust that Sarah could pick it up, but he didn't want to be the one who gave the puck away, so he moved it onto his backhand

and put it hard off the side so it squeaked past the pinching defender and up along the boards.

Sarah read him and swept to the boards, picking up the puck behind the pinching defenceman, who was now caught up-ice.

Dmitri was on the far side. Sarah slapped a hard pass that flew over the remaining defenceman's poking stick and Dmitri knocked it down niftily with his own stick – a "Russian pass," Dimitri called these when the three of them practised high passes in practice. He kicked the falling puck onto his stick and took off, free of any checker.

Travis knew exactly what Dmitri would do – cut across the ice so he was angling into the goal. Fake a forehand to the short side. Keep and tuck around the goalie. Then backhand a shot high.

Sure enough, the water bottle flew off the back of the net just as the red light came on.

Two minutes later Derek knocked down a puck at centre ice and threw a blind pass to Nish, who was charging straight up the middle and hammering his stick on the ice. The pass was almost perfect. Nish reached ahead and just barely poked the puck between the two Detroit defenders, then jumped through and over them as they came together to block him, shooting as he fell. The puck rose hard over the Wheels goaltender's shoulder and Nish came right behind it, knocking the goalie flying as he took out the net. All three – Nish, goalie and, net – crashed into the boards.

Wheels 2, Owls 2.

"Just use your speed," Muck advised at the first break. "It's working."

There were moments when it didn't seem to be working. The Wheels went ahead; Andy tied it up on a great, ripping slapper from the far circle. The Wheels went ahead by two; the Owls tied it again, on a goal by Fahd, on a screen, and by Derek, on a nice tip of a hard Nish screamer from the point. Nish was all business – no show-boating, no Pavel Bure moves, just Nish working as only he could when his mind was on the game.

They finished regulation time tied 5–5. The referee explained there would be a five-minute overtime. If nothing was decided, then the game would go down as a tie; they couldn't go into further overtime, as other teams were scheduled to play. Muck wanted the win. The extra point might make the difference between the Owls making the finals or not.

They played cautiously for the first couple of minutes, each team afraid to make a mistake. Muck played all three lines evenly, hoping for a break that didn't seem to come. The Wheels seemed to be doing the same.

Travis checked the clock. One minute to go. He looked down the bench. Nish was sitting at the far end, his back heaving, his head between

his legs. Not once this game had Nish done anything stupid, not once had he faked an injury,
not once had he even spoken. Travis couldn't
remember a single game where Nish had been
this concentrated.

Muck leaned over Nish and asked him something, Nish nodded, and then Muck slapped his
shoulders. Still fighting for breath, Nish bounded
over the boards for what might be the final faceoff.

"Sarah," Muck called. "Your line."

Travis, too, had yet to recover his breath. But
Sarah and Dmitri were already over the boards.
The faceoff was in the Owls' end, and Sarah was,
by far, the best at faceoffs. They needed to win
this one, to keep it away from the Wheels and to
give themselves one more chance to win.

In one motion Sarah plucked the falling puck
from the air and turned, sticking her rear into
the big Wheels centre so he couldn't get at it.
Travis knew the play perfectly. She would block
and he would scoop up the puck and go.

He grabbed the puck and tucked it away just
as the big centre bulled his way past Sarah.

Nish was behind the net, waiting. Travis fed
him the pass.

The far winger was driving in hard on Nish.
Nish pretended he didn't even see him, then
very gently pinged the puck off the back of the
net just as the winger reached him. There was no
puck for the winger to play, Nish stepped out of

the way, the winger flew past, and Nish easily picked up his own pass as the puck came back to him off the net.

He swung to the far boards, looking up-ice.

Dmitri was breaking. Nish saw him and sent a high, looping pass that almost hit the clock. Dmitri straddled centre to make sure he was onside and pounced as the puck fell.

The Wheels' biggest defenceman was on him, but he was no match for Dmitri's amazing speed. Dmitri shot for the near boards and made as if to cut sharply against the defence for the net. The defence had no choice but to charge full at Dmitri, and Dmitri slipped the puck through his own legs to Sarah, coming up fast with the big centre hacking at her as he tried to keep up.

Travis saw his opening. He cut across towards Dmitri's side and headed in a long curl towards the net. His winger came with him. He could feel the player's stick hard against his shin pads, hard on his pants. He could feel the blade hooking him. The referee should have blown his whistle, but there was nothing. The officials were going to let it go.

Travis attempted to shoot, but the player chasing now had his stick blade right under Travis's arm and was pulling him off the puck. Travis tried again to snap a shot, but he missed the puck and fell. He could hear the crowd yelling for a penalty. But still no whistle.

Travis was down, the checker falling on top of him. Travis kicked at the puck with his skate and it flew back towards the blueline.

With the big Wheels player now fully on top of him, Travis struggled to see.

Nish had the puck!

Nish was in full flight. He picked up the puck at the blueline, and with one lovely little fake to the right he took out the only remaining check. He came in on the goaltender alone.

The goaltender gambled – he rushed at Nish.

Nish pulled the puck back with a perfect little tuck, stepped around the falling, flailing goalie, and, slowly, lifted the puck into the middle of the net.

Owls 6, Wheels 5. The final buzzer could barely be heard above the cheers of the crowd.

Travis scrambled to his feet and charged for Nish, already backing into corner with his stick thrown down and his gloves in the air.

Travis and Sarah and Dmitri hit Nish at the same time, with Sam coming up fast to join in and Jeremy already halfway down the ice and the rest of the Owls pouring over the boards.

"Speed!" Sarah screamed. "SPEEEEEED!"

Nish was smiling at Travis.

"King of Overtime, too," he said. "I forgot that."

11

MR. DILLINGER HAD A TREAT IN STORE FOR THE Owls. He'd booked a section of the new ESPN Zone restaurant just off Times Square. Travis had never seen anything like it: three floors, entirely dedicated to great hamburgers, delicious fries, and wall-to-wall sports. Everywhere he looked there were televisions tuned to sporting events across the world, hundreds of huge screens filled with basketball, football, hockey, soccer from Europe, a Formula One car race from Australia, and, best of all, in the room reserved for the Owls, three sets tuned to the World Junior Hockey Championships in Finland.

Nish strolled in like it was his own living room. He walked to the front row of fat recliner chairs, plunked himself down in the middle seat and called out, "Chips, Coke, burger – no onions, triple ketchup – and the Mighty Ducks versus Detroit, if you don't mind!" One of the waiters, laughing at Nish's nerve, flicked a remote until Nish got exactly what he wanted. Nish pumped a fist in the air in thanks and sank so far into the big seat he all but disappeared from view.

Travis sat at a table with Sarah and Sam and Andy. They ordered onion rings and burgers and were sipping on their Cokes when Sarah, with the straw still in her mouth, nodded towards the far corner.

"Muck's enjoying himself," she muttered, the straw dropping back into the huge glass.

Muck was sitting by himself in the corner, as far removed as possible from the roar of two dozen television sets, each with the volume turned up so loud it sounded like a sports riot was in progress. He had his big arms crossed over his chest and was glowering at one of the screens tuned to the World Juniors.

"Canada losing?" Sam asked.

Sarah shook her head. "Muck hates things like this. Hates sports bars. Hates the way they broadcast games. Remember how he once told us, 'If you can't see it live, you won't see it at all'?"

Travis nodded, giggling at the memory.

"Whazzat supposed to mean?" Sam asked.

"He thinks you can only enjoy a game by seeing the whole thing," explained Travis. "He says things like, 'A camera chasing a puck is as useless as a player chasing the puck.' You know Muck – he thinks the game *away* from the puck is often more interesting than the play around the puck. So he won't watch it on television."

"He's weird," said Sam.

"He's Muck," Andy said, as if in explanation, and it seemed enough for the other three, who all giggled and nodded.

Finally, Muck could take no more. He stood up at his table, drained his Coke, and set the big glass down sharply.

Travis watched as Muck picked up his jacket and tuque and walked over to Mr. Dillinger, who was sitting with Jeremy and Jenny and Derek at another booth. Muck whispered – or perhaps shouted – something in Mr. Dillinger's ear, and Mr. Dillinger nodded and looked up sadly, as if it were somehow all his fault. Muck grinned and rapped the team manager lightly on the arm with a fist. He wasn't upset; the ESPN Zone just wasn't for him. It was perfect for the Screech Owls, though.

They stayed to the end of the Canada–Slovakia game in the World Juniors – the Screech Owls cheering wildly as Canada scored into the empty Slovak net to win 4–2 – and then, their stomachs full and their ears ringing, they paid their bills and headed out again into the street for the walk back to the hotel.

It was snowing again. Large, fat flakes drifted down like feathers between the tall buildings, sparkling as they drifted past the streetlights before joining the snow already lying along the streets and gutters of New York.

It was late, but still it looked like rush hour,

the streets plugged with snow and yellow taxis and police cars and even the odd private vehicle that had failed to heed the week-long warnings to stay out of the downtown core.

The Screech Owls enjoyed the long walk back to the hotel. They tried catching the large flakes in their mouths. They threw snowballs and washed Nish's face and dumped snow down the back of Andy's jacket.

Once they got back, Travis and Sarah caught the first elevator. They held it until Fahd had wheeled Data on, then pushed the button for the second floor. The doors of the old elevator slowly closed, and they rose to the second floor, stopping with a shudder. As they waited for the doors to open, Fahd began stabbing the open button.

"Hold your horses," Travis said, thinking for a moment he must sound like his grandmother, who was always using phrases like that.

"I don't like elevators," said Fahd.

The doors caught, then opened.

Travis blinked in disbelief.

A body lay crumpled on the carpet before them, a large body, wearing a jacket with the collar turned up high so it partially covered the face. A tuque lay to one side.

There was blood oozing from a blow to the back of the man's head.

Sarah screamed.

"MUCK!"

12

"HE COULD'VE BEEN KILLED," SARAH SAID THE next morning.

But Muck had been lucky. His thick tuque had softened the blow to his head. Mr. Dillinger had come back from the hospital with the news that Muck was alert and in good spirits and now had sixteen new stitches to add to his life-time total. "That puts him over three hundred," Mr. Dillinger announced, as if Muck had set a new scoring record. These, however, were the first stitches that hadn't come from playing hockey, whether from a stick, a puck, another player's skate, or the operation Muck had after his leg was broken, putting an end to his junior playing career. What these latest stitches had come from, the police didn't know. No weapon had been found, no one was in custody, no sus-pects were known.

"A mugging," Mr. Dillinger explained. "Hap-pens so often in this city they don't even bother investigating them."

Travis wasn't so sure. A mugging on the second

floor of a downtown Manhattan hotel? Why there, when it would have been so much easier to mug someone walking on the street?

By noon his suspicions had been confirmed.

Muck told the police that he'd gone out to see if he could buy a late theatre ticket, only to find out the storm had shut down the theatre district. He'd walked around a while before returning to the hotel just before the team came back from the restaurant.

Muck's room was on the second floor, same as Data and Fahd's, and when he'd gotten off the elevator and turned towards his room he'd noticed a couple of men struggling with the lock on a room down the hall in the other direction.

Something about the way the men were acting hadn't felt right to Muck, so he pre- tended he'd accidentally turned the wrong way and headed back in their direction, checking the room numbers. When he got there, he real- ized the men were standing outside the room shared by Data and Fahd, the room that con- tained Data's expensive laptop computer.

He figured them for hotel thieves, pretended that he'd just realized he was right the first time, and headed back to his room to call security. He'd barely reached the elevators when some- thing hit him from behind.

The New York police, swamped with traffic problems and other disruptions from the storm, barely managed to send an officer to the hotel. The policeman, who seemed in a hurry to get going, took down what details Muck could supply and said he would file a mugging report. He advised Muck to cancel his credit cards as soon as possible.

"I don't carry any," Muck told him, and the policeman looked at Muck as if the Screech Owls coach came from another planet.

"How much cash did you lose?" the policeman asked.

"Nothing. They took nothing."

The policeman nodded as if the crime had been all but solved. "Scared off," he said knowingly. "You were lucky, mister."

"Lucky to have sixteen stitches and a concussion?" Muck asked, shaking his head. He wasn't impressed.

Travis could make no sense of it all – at least not until Mr. Dillinger happened to read out the description of the men that Muck had given the police. One of the attackers was tall, in a long, dark coat, and wore a multicoloured hat pulled well over his ears, covering much of his face.

Big?

Travis was in his room, lying on his bed watching a "Simpsons" repeat. He was almost asleep when he heard a light tap at the door. It sounded like the housekeeping knock, and he instantly wished he'd remembered to hang the "PRIVACY, PLEASE" sign on the door handle. No one called out, however, and no one tried the handle.

The knock came again, and Travis rolled off the bed and went to see who was there. He needed to get on his tiptoes to see out the spyhole. The fish-eye lens gave a distorted image of the hall, but Travis was glad to have the wide-angle view.

Travis had never seen Fahd's head so big, his nose so long, his eyes so wide and worried. He opened the door quickly. Fahd was there, worry all over his face. Travis first thought something was wrong with Muck. But that wasn't why Fahd had come to call.

"Big was here earlier," Fahd said.

"When?"

"Yesterday. Before we went out. Nish brought him up to the room."

"Your room?"

"Yeah — Data was out with you guys. It was just the three of us. Nish had to show him."

"Show him what?"

"His butt — he wanted Big to see what he was going to do New Year's Eve."

"That's sick!"

"No, no, no, no. He showed him the *recording*. I fired up Data's computer and opened the file so he could see. That's all."

"That's all? That means he knew about the computer. That and the digital camera are worth thousands of dollars."

Fahd seemed on the verge of tears. "But that's just it," he said.

"What do you mean?" asked Travis.

"Nothing was taken. I checked. It's all still there. The computer. The camera. Data was just talking to Lars again about an hour ago."

"Then they couldn't get in the room."

Fahd looked even more upset. "They might have."

Travis was completely alert now. "How do you know? Is something else missing?"

Fahd looked down at his shoes. "My key."

"Your *room* key! How would they get it? You were out at the restaurant with us . . ."

Fahd shook his head. "I couldn't find it when we left. I think maybe someone took it off the dresser earlier in the day." He looked desperately at Travis.

Travis understood. Big had stolen the key earlier when Nish invited him up to the room.

"Then maybe they were coming *out* of the room when Muck came along," said Travis, "not trying to get *in*. We better see if anything's missing."

Fahd nodded. He looked miserable.

Data already knew about the key.

"Nothing else is missing," he announced as Travis and Fahd came in through the door.

"Nothing?" Travis asked to make sure.

"Even the pocket change I left on the dresser is still there. Even" — looking at Fahd — "your stupid fake Oakleys and the Rolex are right there on the desk where you left them."

"And nothing with the computer?" Travis asked.

"Nothing. Everything's still there, exactly as we left it."

"Then maybe Muck did come along just as they were trying to get in," suggested Fahd. "He saved the computer."

But that didn't make sense to Travis. If Muck had come along as they were trying to get in, why wouldn't they just pretend it was the wrong door and move along? Why club Muck on the head if they figured he'd seen nothing?

And if it was just a mugging, as the police contended, why hadn't they stolen his wallet?

It made no sense at all.

13

"*NOT* BIG," NISH MOANED. "NO *WAY* IT WAS HIM."

"Get real," Travis said. "You took him to Data's room. He knew about the computer and the camera. Fahd's room key is missing."

"*But nothing was taken!*"

"Only because Muck came along and spoiled it."

"He's a good guy," Nish protested.

"You don't even know him," Travis said, shaking his head.

"I'm a good judge of people," Nish said. "Even if it was him, he didn't take anything."

"He *hit* Muck!" Travis almost shouted. He couldn't believe Nish wouldn't face facts. But, then again, Travis wasn't at all certain exactly what the facts were in this case.

"Even if it was Big at the door," Nish repeated helplessly, "it doesn't mean he hit Muck." He stood up, reaching for his jacket. "I'm going to find him."

"Who?" Travis asked, not following.

"Big, of course. I'll ask him right to his face."

Travis opened his mouth to speak, but nothing came out. He was stunned.

"*What?*" Nish challenged.

Travis tried again. This time, even though it seemed he had no breath, he was able to speak. "If he tried to kill Muck, who's to say he won't hurt you?"

Nish looked up, not believing Travis could be so foolish as to suggest such a thing. He put his pointer and middle fingers together.

"We're like brothers," Nish said. "Brothers."

"You don't even know his real name," Travis pointed out.

"I trust him with my life," Nish argued.

"That's what I'm afraid of," Travis said, shaking his head.

But Nish wasn't listening. His boots tied and his Screech Owls tuque in hand, he was headed for the door.

"*Wait!*" Travis found himself calling.

Nish stopped at the door, turning expectantly.

"I better come with you," Travis said.

Nish smiled. "I knew you would."

It was growing dark along East 52nd and Lexington. The snow was still falling and, in a surprising way, New York City was gradually beginning to look more like Tamarack than the Big Apple. There was precious little traffic now – only a few yellow cabs and police cars, a front-end loader growling at the end of a street as it dug free an intersection – and the fresh-fallen snow was white and sparkling under the streetlights. For the first time since the Screech Owls had arrived, the city was quiet. Almost peaceful.

Nish was ploughing ahead, head down, into the lightly blowing snow. He walked with determination, each step leaving an ankle-deep hole in the snow.

Travis hurried to keep up. He was fascinated that Nish seemed to know where he was going – a twelve-year-old treating downtown New York City as if it were his own home town – but he had long ago accepted that there were some things in life that Nish understood and many things he did not. While Nish might be able to find his way around the streets of a strange city today, tomorrow he might not be able to find a clean pair of boxer shorts in the mess of clothes dumped at the foot of his bed.

They walked down Lexington and along 42nd past Grand Central Station, which was practically deserted, since no trains had been running for days.

Near Times Square Nish came to a parking lot – cars abandoned by their owners were piled so high with snow it was impossible to tell colour or make – and turned in at an alley leading off it, moving as surely as if he were in his own backyard.

"Where are we going?" Travis asked, trying, but failing, to keep the worry out of his voice.

"Big's been working the streets between Times Square and Rockefeller Center — says it's the only place there's any customers any more. Him 'n' his buds are having a rough go of it."

Travis cringed. "A rough go of it"? How could you feel sorry for a bunch of street crooks selling illegal fake watches?

Travis pointed out the obvious: "This isn't the street. This is an alley."

Nish turned and looked at Travis with contempt. "This is where they operate out of — there's cops all over the streets, in case you haven't noticed."

Nish headed deeper into the alley. It was like entering a room with the lights off. Gone were the streetlights and their warm glow off the snow. It was dark in here, and getting darker. There were footprints everywhere, dark shadows that suggested to Travis they were not alone.

He was losing sight of Nish. The alley twisted up ahead, and Travis hoped it would twist again and then come out on the next street over, but he didn't know for sure. He knew only that he felt uneasy and wished he hadn't come.

He wanted to go back. He opened his mouth to call to Nish, but no sound came out.

Travis couldn't speak for a reason — *there was a large glove clamped over his mouth!*

14

THEY WERE DEEP IN AN UNDERGROUND PARKING lot. Large pipes dripped overhead. The floor was concrete, cracked and stained with salt. The place smelled of grease and exhaust and damp. Several bare bulbs swung from the ceiling at the end of thin electrical cables, sending shadows bouncing against the walls.

Travis had been hustled here so quickly – the stinking glove clamped over his mouth, his right arm locked and pressed behind his back – that only when he was released did he realize Nish had been dragged along too.

There were only a couple of cars in sight. One may have been working; the other certainly was not. It had been stripped of its wheels, and the windshield had been smashed in. The back doors were open and it looked as if someone might have been living in it. There were dirty blankets and old newspapers everywhere.

Along the ledges of the parking garage were stacks of briefcases, like the one Big carried his fake Rolexes in. This had to be "head office" of the fake-watch-and-sunglasses gang, and the two

Owls were clearly considered intruders. Big was nowhere to be seen.

The two large men who had hustled them down here said nothing. They seemed to be waiting for something.

The larger man – heavy, unshaven, with one eye slightly off so it was impossible to tell whether he was looking at Travis or Nish – started at a sound that came from the down-ramp into the garage. He seemed nervous, but at the same time expecting someone.

"*Big!*" Nish suddenly cried out.

There was no fear in his voice. He seemed genuinely glad to see Big walking towards them. And Big, Travis had to admit, seemed glad to see Nish.

"You lookin' for permanent work wit' us, Hockey Man?" Big laughed.

"I knew I'd find you somewhere around here," Nish said. "Dese guys musta t'ought I was da heat."

Big smiled slightly. Travis wondered for a moment exactly how Nish saw himself. Some tough guy who could hold his own with Big and his colleagues? Not likely.

"We have to watch our merchandise, that's all," said Big. "Lots a thieves in da Big Apple, you know."

Yeah, Travis said to himself, and three of them are standing right here.

"What were you after?" Big asked, as if expecting a new order for Oakley sunglasses.

Nish explained. He told about the break-in, or near break-in, at the hotel, and how someone had knocked Muck on the head for sixteen stitches. He said it was Data and Fahd's room, where Big had been invited only a couple of days earlier.

"That's a shame, Hockey Man. Did they get anything?"

As if you need to ask, Travis thought.

"No," Nish said. "Nothing."

"Dat's good," Big said. "Dat's good."

Travis was almost certain Big had glanced quickly at the smaller of the other two men, but he didn't catch any look back and couldn't be sure. Still, he was deeply suspicious.

"Some of da kids think one a da suspects looked like you," Nish said unexpectedly.

Big spun around – to stare at Travis, not Nish. "Peewee here?" he asked.

Nish said nothing, waiting.

Travis cleared his throat.

"M–Muck described something l–like this coat," Travis said.

Big smiled.

"Lots a coats like dis in New York, Peewee. Shadow's got one on right now."

He pointed to the heavy man dressed like himself. Travis never liked the name "Big," but "Shadow" sounded worse.

"Besides," Big continued, "I wasn't any-where near dat place last night. Ain't that right, Shadow?"

Shadow turned, almost as if he hadn't even been listening. He blinked, then answered, "Yah, dat's right. We was at the . . . theatre."

Big nodded. He looked at Nish, waiting for him to respond.

Travis wanted to shout, *Theatre? Right! Sure! Two thugs in long dirty coats and hold-up hats watch-ing a play?*

"Dat's good," said Nish. "I was thinking you might do something like dat."

"We was out all night," said Big. "We got witnesses."

"I'll tell dem," said Nish. "Set dem straight."

"You do dat," Big said. "You do dat."

Nish and Big then changed the topic to watches and sunglasses and how there was nobody around downtown any more to sell to. Nish seemed so sympathetic.

Travis wandered around the parking lot, waiting. He checked out the old abandoned car. Behind it he found a small cache of tinned foods and drinks and even a small cooking unit like the kind campers use. There was garbage every-where. Opened cans. Broken beer bottles.

Why didn't they use the garbage can? Travis wondered. There was a large open drum in the corner that Travis supposed was for trash.

He wandered over and looked in. It was a firepit. There were black ashes halfway to the top, and charred broken boards, some with nails still in them. They had the camper stove for cooking, Travis knew. They must set fires here for heat. He hated to think of such a life.

Travis could tell by the sounds that Nish was getting ready to head back to the hotel. He was just about to step away from the rear of the car when he looked in on the dashboard, beneath the crumbling windshield.

A hotel-room key!

Fahd's missing key?

15

WHAT WAS WRONG WITH EVERYONE? TRAVIS wondered.

First, Nish had refused to listen to him on the long trudge through the snow back to the hotel. He wouldn't believe for a moment that the key was Fahd's. What proof did Travis have? he wanted to know. The key had no number on it. It didn't even have the name of the hotel on it. It could be anyone's, said Nish, even Big's.

Sure, Travis wanted to say, Big really lives in a fancy hotel and just sells fake watches and hangs around underground parking garages for fun.

Travis was disappointed in his friend, but that was nothing compared to how he felt after he got off the telephone with the New York police. He'd managed to track down the policeman who'd investigated Muck's "mugging," but the man seemed absolutely uninterested in the case. Hotel keys were a dime a dozen, he said to Travis. People lost them all the time. Seeing a key in an old car didn't mean a thing. Nor had the policeman seemed interested in Travis's description of Big and Shadow and how one of them might have been the guy who clubbed Muck.

"Son," the policeman said in a way that made Travis feel five years old, "a million people in this city might fit that description. Call me back when you get a signed confession."

Travis lay on his bed staring at the ceiling. Perhaps the police were right. Someone may or may not have been in Data's and Fahd's room, but even if they had, nothing was taken. Someone did club Muck, but nothing had been taken from him, either. Perhaps Nish was right, too. Big wasn't involved. Perhaps, for that matter, Big and Shadow *had* been at the theatre the other night – a musical, maybe, with the two of them standing at the encore to toss bouquets of flowers at the stars.

But somehow Travis didn't think so.

The Owls had a game to play. Travis was disgusted with himself; he'd become so caught up in the world of crime and police investigations that he'd almost forgotten why the Screech Owls were in New York City.

They were in the middle of a big tournament. And they'd need Travis, the captain, concentrating on hockey if they were going to have a chance of winning.

They were to play a team from Chicago, the

Young Blackhawks, in the same small rink where they'd played their opener. No Madison Square Garden again until they made the final — if they made the final.

The Blackhawks were a good, smart team — well coached, big, and mean. They caught the Owls off guard early, and within a matter of minutes the score was 2–0 for the Chicago peewees on only four shots. Jenny, whose turn it was to play nets this game, was also struggling.

"You're quicker than they are," Muck said to them before the next faceoff. "Better to be fast than big. Remember the last game."

Dmitri got the Owls rolling first, with a fast dash up-ice to beat the Chicago defenceman back to a puck that just came short of icing. He pulled around the defender, scooped up the puck, and set up behind the Blackhawk net, looking for someone coming in.

Travis came in hard from the left side, Sarah down the middle. Dmitri faked to Travis and hit Sarah, who shot immediately, the puck bouncing high off the goaltender's shoulder and fluttering in the air as it fell back to the ice.

It never made it. Travis's stick flashed in front of the goaltender and picked the puck, baseball-style, out of mid-air and sent it into the far side of the net.

"Great play!" Sarah said as they mobbed Travis in the corner.

"Lucky, lucky," Nish kidded as he poked a glove through the scrum and smacked the top of Travis's helmet.

Travis grinned. He knew Nish was closer to the truth than Sarah, but he had meant to hit the puck, and it worked. It must have looked great.

The Owls tied it in the second period when Sam made a great rush up-ice. Just as she drew the Chicago defence in to check her, she flipped a backhand across-ice that little Simon Milliken picked up and rapped off the post. The rebound went to Andy, who hammered a shot that the falling Chicago goaltender barely managed to stop, and Mario, the ultimate garbage collector, was there to pick up the loose puck and lift it into the net.

Heading into the final minute, the two teams were still tied, with four goals each. Travis knew how badly they needed the win. It would give them a perfect record, and probably put them into the finals. A tie might leave it up in the air. A loss could mean elimination.

He skated quickly by Nish as they lined up for the next faceoff. "We win, we play in MSG again," he said quietly as he brushed past.

Travis knew what those words would do to Nish. Nish would see himself back at Madison Square Garden. The championship game. A big crowd. Television. David Letterman. Nish scoring his "Pavel Bure." A Hollywood contract. Action figures of Wayne Nishikawa under every Christmas tree. Dates with supermodels. Nish so famous he'd need *real* Oakleys to hide behind so he wouldn't be mobbed – which would happen anyway, of course.

The puck dropped. Sarah took out her check and Dmitri picked up the puck and flipped it back to Sam, who was on with Nish for the final minute of play. Sam fired it cross-ice to Nish, who took the pass at full stride. He was over the blue-line and headed for centre when he fired a quick, unexpected pass that flew by Travis's left shoulder.

What's he doing? Travis wondered.

But then he saw. The Blackhawk defenceman had moved up tight on Travis, setting for a turnover. He had clearly hoped to dive past Travis and knock the puck away and free, but Nish's high pass had caught the defenceman completely by surprise. He was back on his heels, and when he tried to turn he fell.

The puck pounded into the boards and dropped to the ice, bouncing out perfectly as Travis sidestepped the falling defenceman and headed in on net.

Dmitri hammered his stick on the ice, looking for the pass. Travis hit him perfectly just as the far defenceman was turning for Travis, leaving Dmitri alone. Dmitri came in, faked, and dropped a long blind pass that landed perfectly on Sarah's stick.

The Chicago centre dived, hoping to take Sarah's skates out from under her. But Sarah was ready. She dropped the puck again, just as the Blackhawks centre tackled her and took her down.

The referee's hand went up – but the whistle couldn't go until a Chicago player touched the puck.

Sam picked it up in full flight.

Dmitri rapped his stick on the side of the net.

The Chicago goalie tried to play both Dmitri and Sam at the same time.

Sam shot, a hard slapper, that blew past the goalie on the blocker side, high and in off the elbow where the post meets the crossbar.

A moment, barely, before the horn blew to end regulation play.

Screech Owls 5, Young Blackhawks 4.

The players on the ice were first to mob Sam. Then the rest of the Owls and Muck arrived, slipping and falling along the ice.

"*What a play!*" Sarah was screaming.

"*Awesome!*" shouted Dmitri. "*Great shot, Sam!*"

"I set it all up," whined Nish. "And I won't even get credit for an assist."

Block him out, Travis told himself. Just block him out.

16

IT WAS THE LAST DAY OF THE YEAR. FROM THE way the snow was still falling — huge flakes that built into drifts, the side streets of New York now impassable — it felt like it might be the last day of forever. The dawn of a new Ice Age.

The New Year's Eve celebrations had not been cancelled. They had become, instead, a bigger story than usual — the people of New York City gathering at Times Square as a kind of declaration of solidarity against the elements. It could snow all it wanted; the storm was not going to stop the countdown to midnight.

They were now predicting a record number of people in Times Square. And the occasion had become an international news story; there might be as many as *two billion* people tuning in from around the world — the largest television audience since the first moon landing back in 1969!

"How appropriate," Nish announced with delight. "Both times they'll be tuning in to see a moon."

Not only was Nish still going to proceed with his outrageous plan, but Data and Fahd had become almost as caught up in the scheme themselves.

Data had swept the Internet for information on how to hack into a broadcast line. Travis was amazed at how much information was readily available through chat lines and Web sites. Data had been able to verify that a live, on-location broadcast like this would be done through the phone lines. They already had Data's laptop computer. They had the file containing Nish's moon. They had a telephone line at the hotel and, if they really needed it, a connection to Fahd's cell-phone that would allow them to do it all from Times Square itself.

But they still needed more technical information. It was one thing to know the broadcaster, Data told them, but quite another to get to the video boards that would be controlling the broadcast. It would take them hours, if it could be done at all, to hack through the broadcaster's telephone system to reach the right location to begin their work. Considering the blocks and passwords that were likely involved, the task was next to impossible.

Data, however, had found a contact in Germany who kept e-mailing new ideas for them to try, and within an hour of computer time they had their answers.

"We can get the number for the direct phone line off the broadcast truck," Data explained. "Each truck has the number listed on the outside. We need to get the number for the main truck, then we're just one password away from the control board — and passwords tend to be obvious. We can worry about that later — right now we need the number from that truck."

"Let's go!" Andy shouted.

Travis might be team captain, but he was certainly not in charge here. The idea of Nish mooning the entire world had captured everyone's imagination. All he could do was go along for the ride — and be there if he was needed.

They told Mr. Dillinger they were just slipping over to Times Square to see what the preparations were like. There were six of them altogether — Fahd, Nish, Andy, Derek, Jesse, and Travis. Mr. Dillinger told them to be careful, to stick together, and not to get in anyone's way. They promised, and set out through the drifting snow.

The stage was almost ready when they got there. This was where the host would be doing the countdown. A huge ball was going to fall down a spiral high on one of the towers precisely at midnight, and the whole ceremony would be flashed live on the big screen above the square at the same time it was broadcast across the world.

The broadcast trucks were parked up a side street just away from the stage area, but there was crowd-control fencing blocking the way, and security everywhere.

"How are we going to get it?" Andy asked.

"We'll never get past that cop," said Fahd.

"We can talk to him," Jesse said. "He looks bored anyway."

"What about?" Fahd asked.

"Nothin'," said Derek. "Just ask him some stupid questions – keep him busy while one of us slips through."

"Who'll ask him questions?" Fahd wondered.

All five of the other Owls were staring at him. They needed stupid questions. They needed someone who could ask questions all day long if necessary. And there was only one Owl for that job: Fahd.

"Okay," Fahd said. "And who's going to get the number?"

"It'll need to be someone who won't be noticed," Andy said. "Someone smaller."

Now they all turned and stared at Travis. If it required someone small, there was only one Owl for that job.

Travis nodded okay. He didn't think he could speak.

Fahd performed brilliantly. The policeman seemed to enjoy talking to kids. He was fascinated that they had come here from Canada, and he wanted to know if any of them knew a cousin he had up there somewhere.

"In Victoria, I think," he said. "Something to do with a queen, anyway. He's got a wheat farm or something."

"Regina," Fahd offered. "You must mean Regina. It's in Saskatchewan."

"Whatever," the cop said, and switched to a subject he liked better – himself. For a long time he talked about being a policeman in New York City, while the Owls listened and kicked up mounds of snow with the toes of their boots. But slowly Fahd got him onto the topic of the upcoming show.

Fahd played him perfectly. Flattered, the policeman began talking like a television executive. He used the star's first name as if they were best of friends. He talked about rehearsals and make-up artists and how important his own job was.

"Where does the director sit?" Fahd asked.

"Well," the cop said, "it's not like the movies. There's no director's chair, and he doesn't wear a French beret and shout through a bullhorn. In fact, there might be three or four directors. They work from that big truck back there."

Fahd and the others craned their necks to see.

"Which one?" Fahd asked.

The policeman looked back as if to make sure himself. "The blue one. The one right dead below the portable satellite dish."

Fahd looked quickly at Travis, who understood. Travis would need to get away now if he got the chance.

"Is that gun loaded?" Fahd asked, nodding at the policeman's open holster.

The cop laughed. "'Course it's loaded, son – you don't think we fight bad guys with water pistols, now, do you?"

"Yeah, but," Fahd said, "in Canada they have to load them first. And they're all holstered up practically out of sight."

"Canada ain't New York City, kid," the cop said, as if they hadn't realized. "If I took the time to unbuckle and load up, I'd be shot a thousand times before I was ready."

The policeman was off and running. He began to brag about the cases he'd solved and the drug dealers he'd arrested and the important people he'd guarded – never for a moment aware that a bunch of twelve-year-olds had just pulled the wool so far over his eyes he was about to flunk the one assignment he had that day: keeping people out.

Travis slipped away and ducked under the nearest truck. He wriggled his way through to a narrow space between one truck with "MAKE-UP" on it and another with "MAIN FEED," all the time keeping an eye out for security.

Someone had left deep tracks in the snow, and he kept to them, careful not to leave his own small footprints behind.

As Travis drew closer to his goal he heard a man cough. He leaped from the footprints and scrambled under the nearest truck, rolling in the snow.

Just in time! Two television-crew members rounded the far corner and walked down the same narrow space he'd been coming through.

Travis rolled out the other side of the truck, retraced his steps, and, when the men had gone – thank heavens for coughs! – he stepped back out into the tracks and hurried the rest of the way.

"DIRECTOR" a sign read on the blue vehicle's side. The policeman had been right.

"MAIN CONTROL PANEL," it read below. And beneath that was a number: 212-555-7449.

Travis stared hard at the number. *How would he ever remember all that?* He had nothing to write it down with. He couldn't write it in the snow – what good would that do? He *had* to remember it.

The first part – 212 – was the area code. Even if he forgot that, he could easily look it up.

The second part was also a snap. 555 – he'd seen enough television shows to know that was always the number in these circumstances!

But 7449?

Easy – Travis Lindsay, Wayne Nishikawa, and Sarah Cuthbertson. Numbers 7, 44, and 9.

He raced back along the tracks through the snow, repeating the numbers out loud as he hurried to where the policeman was just winding up yet another story of a mob shootout.

17

"WE HAVE TO DO A DRY RUN FIRST," DATA SAID.

Fahd nodded. He understood. The others were not so sure. As soon as they were back in the hotel, Travis had carefully written down the numbers – mumbling as he did so, 2-1-2, 5-5-5, me-Nish-Sarah" – and though Fahd had looked at him a little oddly, he'd taken the slip of paper and handed it to Data.

"Whadya mean 'a dry run'?" Nish practically shouted. "You think I'm gonna wet my pants at a time like this?"

The others ignored him and set about hooking up the system. They connected the computer to the phone line, used a double jack to connect the telephone itself, and Fahd and Data began calling up their program.

"What's the number again?" Data asked.

Fahd spun the paper so Data could see as he typed it into the computer. There was a pause and then, quickly, a series of notes as the computer dialled.

No one dared take a breath while they waited.

There was a long, seemingly too long, hiss, then some loud clicks and buzzes, then silence.

"*We're in!*" Data said in a voice somewhere between a whisper and a hiss.

The logo of the broadcaster came up first on Data's screen, and then a small box, empty, with the cursor pulsating in the corner. "PASSWORD," it said above the box.

"Now's the tough part," said Data.

Fahd held his hands over the keyboard, his fingers dancing in the air.

"*What is it?*" Fahd kept saying. "*What is it? What is it?*"

"Probably the director's name," said Andy.

"Nah," said Data. "It would be a code word. Something they wouldn't forget."

"The date?" Jesse suggested.

"I like it," Fahd said, and immediately typed in the date.

They waited a moment while the screen faded, then bounced back.

"PASSWORD FAILURE," the screen said. "PLEASE TRY AGAIN."

"Be careful," Data said. "Probably three mistakes and it closes down. There might even be an alert on it."

"The name of the host?" Derek suggested.

"That might be it!" said Fahd. He typed the host's name in and then pressed ENTER.

The screen faded and then reappeared.

"PASSWORD FAILURE. PLEASE TRY AGAIN."

"Last chance," Data muttered. He sounded ready for defeat.

"*Happy New Year*," said Nish miserably. He sounded as if his world had just come to an end.

Fahd turned around quickly. "What was that?"

"What was what?" Nish said, not following.

"What you just said."

"Happy New Year?"

"That could be it!" Fahd said. "That's probably it."

"Type it in," Data said.

Fahd's fingers flew over the keys. He hit ENTER, and again the page on the screen vanished. This time, however, it did not come back right away saying they had failed. When the screen returned it said something different.

"NEW YEAR'S SPECIAL."

Fahd pumped a fist over his head. "You did it, Nish! You're a *genius!*"

"It took you till now to find that out?" Nish said. But he was red-cheeked and smiling, astonished at his own lucky guess.

Files began appearing on the screen.

"What're those?" Andy asked.

"Should be everything," Data said. "Even the commercial breaks. Everything that isn't live is right here as a pre-recorded file, and all it takes is a double click to load it up onto the big screen."

"How do I get my butt up there?" Nish asked. His voice was a bit whiney, as if he resented no longer being the centre of attention, the glory going, for the moment, to Data and Fahd, who had hacked their way into the broadcast.

"Simple," explained Data. "I just insert your file into the list and double-click when we want it up. It overrides everything."

"From here?" Nish asked.

"From here," Data said.

"I get to moon the world and I don't even have to leave my hotel room to do it?"

"You got it, Einstein."

"Beauty," Nish said. "Beauty."

Just then there was a loud rap at the door.

Everyone froze.

18

FOR A LONG MOMENT, NO ONE DARED MOVE.

The sharp knock on the door seemed to echo through the room, though it had not been repeated.

"*Who is it?*" Fahd hissed. "Check it out!"

Andy, the tallest, crept silently to the door. He stood up straight and cautiously put his eye to the peep-hole.

He turned, smiling. "It's Sarah and Sam."

Fahd, who had already cut the connection and was in the process of turning off his computer, lifted his hand off the keys and relaxed. "Let them in," he said.

Sarah and Sam burst into the room, filling it with new energy.

"Smells like a hockey dressing room in here," Sam said. "Whatya been sweatin' over, Rolex Boy?" She poked Nish in the gut. He buckled over, pretending she'd winded him.

"What's going on?" Sarah asked. "Nish headed into the *Guinness Book of World Records* or what?"

"We're in," Fahd said. "He's almost there."

"*The entire world's gonna hurl!*" Sam shouted.

"Very funny," muttered Nish. "Very, very funny."

"I want to know how you're going to do it," Sarah said to Data and Fahd.

They were delighted to explain. They walked Sarah and Sam through all the technical details and described, with due credit to Nish, how they'd cracked the password that took them straight into the computer controls of the broad-cast truck.

"Nish's butt is just a double click away from being seen around the world," said Data. "He's going to make history."

"I'll believe it when I see it," said Sam. "I don't even believe he mooned for you guys."

"*Did so!*" Nish all but shouted.

"Prove it!" Sam challenged.

She had Nish in the palm of her hand. Less than a year on the Screech Owls and Sam could work Nish better than anyone, playing him like a puppet on a string.

"Show them!" Nish commanded Data and Fahd.

"What?" Fahd asked. "The file?"

"My butt," corrected Nish.

"Show us," Sam said. "You're going to show everybody later, anyway. Surely you can give two young women a sneak preview of the Eighth Wonder of the World!"

"C'mon," said Sarah. "Give us a look so we'll know what it is when it comes up on the screen."

"Okay," Data said.

Fahd went into the directory until he found the file marked "Moonshot," then double-clicked on it. The machine whirred and hummed, stopped and started, whirred and hummed some more.

"It's a big file," Data explained.

"It's a big butt," Sam replied.

The screen flashed, then filled with a man's face.

He was wearing a ski mask, pulled down tight over his face.

"*What the hell?*" Nish shouted.

"Wrong file," Fahd said to Data.

"No," Data said. "It's the right file. Something's wrong."

The camera pulled out from the man in the ski mask. He was flanked by two other men, each dressed the same: long dark coat, gloves, ski mask over the face exposing only the eyes.

Each man was carrying an automatic rifle pointed directly at the camera.

The man in the middle began to speak. It was rough — computer data becoming sound — but it was clear and to the point.

"BE PREPARED TO DIE, NEW YORKERS!" the voice shouted slowly and deliberately. "AT MIDNIGHT WE KILL ANYONE STILL ON THE STREETS!"

The man turned his weapon and shot several rounds to the side of the camera. The shots sounded tinny over the small speakers of Data's laptop, but to Travis they sounded like exploding bombs.

"BE PREPARED TO DIE!"

Travis felt a deep, sickening chill down his spine. They were terrorists. Terrorists threatening to gun down anyone attending the New Year's Eve celebrations in Times Square.

"*Who are they?*" Sam asked, giggling slightly as if hoping it might be some elaborate practical joke.

Travis figured he knew. He had recognized the voice.

19

TRAVIS HADN'T BEEN THE ONLY ONE TO recognize the voice. As soon as he looked at Nish and saw his beet-red, sweating face, he knew that Nish, too, had realized instantly who was beneath the balaclava.

Big.

Nish took it particularly badly. Not just because the lead terrorist turned out to be his great friend, but because his ambitious plan to moon the entire world had gone up in smoke.

Travis could tell that Nish was struggling with what to do. There was little choice, however.

"We better show this to somebody," Travis said.

Nish nodded helplessly.

Travis led the little group down to Mr. Dillinger's room. Mr. Dillinger called in Muck while the Owls explained the situation. Fahd then played the recording for them both.

Mr. Dillinger called the police. A detective came and heard the story and, once again, Fahd played the recording. The police demanded that the Screech Owls take them to this man called

104

Big, and Nish sadly led the way to the underground garage where he had last met with his
great friend.

Travis was astonished at how quickly the
police moved. In no time, with the Owls well
out of the way, they had gathered up Big and his
buddies and hauled them off to be charged.

"What for?" Nish asked.

The detective in charge looked at him as if it
were one of the stupidest questions he had ever
heard. "Uttering terrorist threats," he said. "In
this country, that's right up there with murder."

One of Big's friends had broken immediately
and explained the story.

It was all Big's idea. He'd got it when Nish
had invited Big over to the hotel room to tell
him about his great scheme to moon the world.
Big had even been shown the file of Nish
mooning before the camera.

Big was smarter than Travis had imagined. He
had figured out that if he could just replace the
"Moonshot" file on the computer with another
one, then instead of Nish's big butt on the screen
at Times Square the New Year's crowd would see
his own recording.

"This man claims there was no real terrorist
threat," the detective said. "The guy they all call
Big figured that they could panic the crowd
who'd come down to see the show. With everyone running for cover, and with the snowstorm

still blowing, they'd paralyze the city and empty the downtown core, leaving them free to loot wherever they wanted – even along Fifth Avenue.

"They filmed their own recording and saved it on disk. It took them less than five minutes to break into the hotel room, replace your file with theirs, and give it the same name. That way, you would load their file thinking it was yours. It was pretty ingenious – and it might have worked if you hadn't checked it out first."

"So it *was* them who hit Muck!" Sarah said.

The detective nodded. "There's also going to be assault charges," he said. "These guys are in deep trouble, believe me."

"But–but–but," Nish began, "what happened to my file?"

"It's gone," the detective said. "Outer space, I guess. But count yourself lucky, son."

"W–why's that?"

"If your file had gone up on that screen, I might be here charging you instead."

Nish stuck out his chin, challenging. "No way you'd have recognized me."

The policeman blew out his cheeks and shook his head. "We'd have checked every butt in New York," he said. "A butt like that is pretty distinctive, wouldn't you say?" He pointed at Nish's rear end.

Nish blazed red – for once speechless.

20

NEW YEAR'S EVE IN TIMES SQUARE WAS wonderful. The snow stopped falling, the ploughs came out and cleared off the main streets, and downtown New York filled with hundreds of thousands of New Year's revellers. The noise was deafening, the countdown and the fireworks spectacular. The broadcast went off without a hitch. No terrorist threats. No bare bum.

Nish was shattered. He walked around with his hands deep in his pockets and his face so sad you'd think his life was coming to an end. When the great ball dropped and the New Year arrived, he would have nothing to do with noisemakers. He wouldn't dance. He wouldn't cheer. He wouldn't look at the big screen.

"My one chance to make the *Guinness Book of World Records,*" he kept muttering. "And I blew it."

"Get into the spirit, Rolex Boy," Sarah told him. "It's a whole new year — *anything* can happen."

"Nothin' that good," Nish said despondently. "That was the single greatest idea I ever had in my life. It's all downhill from here for me."

Sarah spun her finger by her temple and rolled her eyes at Travis. Travis shrugged. Nish was just being Nish. By tomorrow he'd have forgotten all about it and have a brand-new idea.

"Better get to bed," Mr. Dillinger said as he came up behind them. "We're on at noon tomorrow. Madison Square Garden. Championship game."

"Who are we playing?" asked Derek.

"The Detroit Wheels," Mr. Dillinger said. "We came first, they were right behind us in the standings."

"The Wheels?" Nish asked. "Was that the team I scored the winner against?"

Mr. Dillinger frowned and looked over his glasses at Nish. How could he have forgotten? But Travis knew Nish hadn't forgotten for a second. He just wanted to remind everyone he had scored the winner.

Nish was back in the real world.

21

EVERYTHING HAD CHANGED. NO ONE WAS talking any more about hacking into a broadcast. Nish wasn't going on about his butt or the *Guinness Book of World Records*. He was, instead, sitting fully dressed in the visitors' dressing room of Madison Square Garden, his head resting on his shin pads, deep in concentration. He hadn't even bothered to check out the photographs in the hallway. He had come to do one thing – play hockey.

"You know what you need to do," Muck said just before he opened the door that led to the ice surface. "Go to it."

Travis smiled to himself as he strapped on his helmet. For Muck, that almost amounted to a major speech. Nothing about how far they'd come together, nothing about armies fighting glorious battles, no fancy quotes that no one could understand – just good old Muck, telling them to get out there and "Go to it."

They headed onto the ice, Jeremy first, spinning at the blueline so he skated backwards into the net, where he immediately began scraping the ice so he could rough up his crease. He seemed oblivious to his surroundings. How Jeremy could fail to notice there were several thousand people in the stands, Travis didn't know.

Travis skated around on the new ice, feeling his legs. Sarah was up ahead, gliding smoothly as she took her turn around the back of the net. Nish was pounding Jeremy's pads like they were some horrible animal that had to be killed before the game could begin. Everything was in order for the Screech Owls. Travis even hit the crossbar during warm-up. He felt great. He knew that this game, this championship match in the Big Apple International Peewee Tournament, was going to be a great one.

The people had come out of curiosity. The snowstorm was over, and the downtown streets were slowly returning to normal, but the people of New York were still essentially stranded in their city. There was little else to do but go for a walk, ski in the park, or find something like a minor-hockey tournament to take in. Madison Square Garden had opened its doors and was charging nothing. This and the television coverage the various teams had been given during the storm combined to bring thousands out to see the final match.

Muck was right. There was nothing he needed to say about the Wheels. They were big, and seemingly older than the Owls. They had great shots, and could score goals. The two teams were almost perfectly matched, with the Screech Owls' speed and skill at playmaking roughly equalled by the Wheels' strength and shots. The two teams had already played once to sudden-death overtime. It was going to be a great final.

Sarah's line started, with Nish and Fahd back on defence. Sarah took the opening faceoff easily and sent Dmitri flying down the wing so fast he caught a slow Detroit defender off guard, set him back on his heels, and tore past him for a quick snap shot that ticked off the post – and then off the glass.

It might have been 1–0 for the Owls but for a fraction of an inch. The puck bounced off the glass, jumped over Nish's stick as he pinched in, and immediately the Wheels were off on a two-on-one with only Fahd back.

Travis knew what he had to do. Sarah and Dmitri were both caught up-ice. He was behind the play, but he had the angle on the puck carrier and had better speed. He dug down so hard he felt his lungs burn with the effort. He tucked low to the ice and tried to flick his ankles with every push off, anything for more speed.

The two Wheels were over the blueline with Fahd between them. Travis noticed the puck carrier look for his partner.

Travis gambled that he would pass.

Jumping with one final push, Travis flew through the air and landed flat on his chest, with his stick held out in front of him in one hand.

The pass was already on the way, hard and perfectly aimed at the tape of the second Wheel, who pulled his stick back to one-time it.

Travis reached as far as he could, his arm seeming almost to unhinge. He felt the puck just tick the toe of his stick blade, then heard the whistle as the puck flew over the boards and out of play. He kept sliding, right through the circle and into the boards.

The other Owls on the ice raced to him as if he'd scored.

"*Great play, Trav!*" Sarah called.

"*You saved a goal!*" Fahd shouted.

Nish said nothing. But when Travis got to his knees, he felt a quick, light tap on the seat of his hockey pants. His old friend, being grateful.

The game surged end to end, with great attacks and even greater defensive plays. Sam blocked a shot from the slot that would have gone in had she not thrown herself in front of it. Nish broke up rush after rush. Andy checked the top Detroit centre to a standstill. Jeremy was brilliant, making glove saves and pad saves, dropping down into the butterfly to prevent wraparounds, and once stopping a hard shot from the point with his mask, a shot so hard it ripped the mask clean off.

At the other end, Travis hit the crossbar – only this time it didn't make him smile. The Wheels goalie stopped Dmitri on a clean break and stopped Wilson on a great pinch from the point.

"It's coming," Muck said at the first break. "It's coming."

In the second period, both teams scored early, the Wheels on a lucky tip that went off Wilson's skate, the Owls when Mario picked up one of his specialties, a garbage goal, after Nish had sent a hard drive into the crease and the goaltender let the rebound slip away.

Sarah scored on a pretty play where she slipped the puck through a Detroit defender's feet and then pulled out the goalie. The Wheels came back on a breakaway when Fahd let his man beat him to the outside. Derek scored on a hard blast from the top of the circle. The Wheels scored on the power play after Andy had been sent off for tripping.

It was a tie game, Wheels 3, Owls 3, with one period left to play.

They flooded the ice between the second and third periods, and the Owls returned to their dressing room to wait. Nish threw a towel over his head and hid his face beneath it. He was fully concentrating now.

Travis was glad Nish hadn't noticed the camera crew walking through the crowd and shooting the action on the ice. He knew if Nish saw a TV camera, he'd become a different player from the one they so desperately needed right now.

Muck and Mr. Dillinger came into the room, Muck holding a single sheet of paper in both hands, low, and staring at it as if he could not quite believe what he was reading.

"Different rules for the championship game," Muck announced. "Five minutes of sudden-death overtime if it's still tied after three. Then a shoot-out. You know what I think about shootouts."

Muck hated them. Hockey, he always said, was a *team* game, not an exhibition of individual skills. But then, he didn't like the designated hitter in baseball, either. The Owls, on the other hand, dreamed of shootouts, and the glory that would come from scoring a spectacular goal.

Late in the third, Muck's fears looked as if they might be coming true. The Owls had scored on a lucky tip by Simon Milliken, but the Wheels had tied it 4–4 on another power play.

Travis could sense the game slowing. He had to admit, Muck had a point. If teams knew there would be a shootout, they tended to play *for* the shootout, counting on their best players to win it when no one was checking them.

Travis had never been checked so tightly. It was almost as if another player was inside his sweater with him, pulling him here and pushing him there. Every time he tried to escape into open ice, he felt an arm across his chest, a hook inside his elbow, a stick between his legs.

It was the same for everyone. Sarah couldn't find the space she needed for plays, Dmitri couldn't find the open ice he needed for his speed.

The Wheels checked frantically, but when they had the puck, they made no effort to carry it up-ice towards the Screech Owls' goal. Instead, they dumped it deep into the Owls' end – forcing Jeremy to leave his net to play it – then ran for the bench and a change rather than chase the puck in and try to cause a turnover.

They were in the dying minutes of a championship, and Travis had never seen the game played so methodically, so predictably. Muck was right about shootouts.

The buzzer sounded to signal the end of regulation time, and the players gathered at the bench, Nish flicking the cap off a water bottle and dumping it all down the back of his neck. They were exhausted, and now they had to face five minutes of sudden-death hockey. There would be no flood. They would play the five minutes on the same ice surface, rutted and snowy, very much to the advantage of the slower, larger Detroit team.

"Try to end it early," Muck said to Sarah's line. "I don't want us in a shootout."

Sarah won the faceoff, but the Detroit centre all but tackled her when she tried for the loose puck. Travis found himself wrestling with the opposite winger and couldn't get to it either. Sarah tried to slip around her check and was pitchforked over, crashing and sliding towards the far boards.

Travis caught Sarah's expression as she turned. She was staring icicles at the referee, but the ref, who had been standing right beside the two centres when the big Detroit player had dumped her, was acting as if nothing at all had happened.

If Muck hated shootouts, Travis hated officials who treated third periods and overtimes as if they were different from the rest of the game.

"I can't move out there!" Sarah said when they came off.

"I know," Travis said. "It's crazy."

Travis felt a knock on the side of his shin pad. It was Nish, reaching for him down the bench with his stick.

"If I get a chance," Nish said, his face soaked with sweat and beaming red, "I'm carrying. You cover."

Travis nodded.

Next shift Sarah tried a new tactic. Instead of going for the puck as usual, she ignored it and took out the big Detroit centre, very nearly pitchforking him back as she used her strength to leverage him off the puck.

Holding off the centre with her back, Sarah kicked the puck towards Travis, who darted in under his own check to sweep it away and against the boards.

Finally, a little space!

Travis turned, picked up the puck, and headed for the back of the Owls' net. The far winger was coming hard at him, and Travis faked a shot against the boards and simply left the puck behind the net, throwing his shoulder into the checker and sending him off balance out into the slot area.

Nish was there to pick up the drop. He stick-handled easily, checking both sides.

Sarah cut straight across the ice towards the middle. Two Wheels stuck to her, both hooking.

Nish held, and when the free Detroit forward came at him, he tapped it off the back of the net so it bounced right back to him as the checker flew by.

Nish had the open left side, and took it. He moved up-ice quickly. Travis bumped the player closest to him to give Nish more room, and Sarah, the cleanest player on the team, used her stick to hold back the big Detroit centre.

Nish kept over the Wheels' blueline. Travis remembered what he had been told – "You cover!" – and dropped back into Nish's spot to be in position to defend against any turnover.

Nish faked a pass to Dmitri and still held. There was no lane to the net. He stayed along the boards and stopped abruptly as a Detroit defenceman came in hard with his shoulder. The checker missed, crashed into the boards and crumpled to the ice.

Nish was still looking to pass. The big centre had Sarah tied up. Dmitri was stapled to the far boards by an interfering backchecker. Travis was back, just outside the blueline to cover a quick break the other way, so Nish couldn't risk a pass to him that might go offside. Fahd was on the far side, but a cross-ice pass would be too risky.

Nish worked back of the Wheels' net, stick-handling easily as he tried to read the situation.

Everywhere he looked, Screech Owls players were tied up. He, however, was free; the player who'd slammed into the boards was still trying to pick up his stick with his big, clumsy gloves on.

Travis could not believe what he was seeing. It was almost as if he saw it all happen even before Nish pulled back the puck so it flipped up onto the blade of his stick.

He's not!

But he was. The puck cradled flat on his blade, Nish casually tossed it high so that it sailed over the top of the net like a golf ball lobbed out of a sand trap.

With no one on him, Nish furiously moved his legs so he came spinning around the front of the net just as the puck landed, flat, in the slot. He was still unchecked, the player who'd lost his stick only now diving, stick in hand, in the hopes of blocking the shot.

He was too late. Nish picked the top corner, blew it over the goaltender's glove, and punched the water bottle so hard off the back of the net it hit the glass and sprayed all over it, right in front of the goal judge.

The red light came on.

The Screech Owls had won in sudden-death over-time!

And Nish had scored his Pavel Bure goal!

22

TRAVIS WASN'T EXACTLY SURE WHEN NISH HAD first noticed the cameras. He couldn't have missed the crews running onto the ice to film the Owls piling on top of him. But it seemed to Travis that Nish must have seen them earlier; why else would he have tried his crazy play? Travis didn't much care. It had worked. Nish had his Pavel Bure goal – and the Owls had the championship.

Nish put on a humble act when the cameras closed around him and the reporters began peppering him with questions. He called it a "lucky play" and gave credit to his teammates, but Travis didn't believe it for a moment. Nish was in his glory.

"Maybe Letterman will call," Sam said sarcastically as the rest of the Owls stood around watching Nish fielding questions.

"Guinness won't be," said Sarah, giggling.

She was right. Nish might have come to New York to moon – but instead he'd ended up a star.

After Travis had accepted the trophy, and medals were being presented to both teams, he noticed the camera crews talking with the organizers. Then just when it seemed he should pick up the trophy and hold it over his head for a victory lap of Madison Square Garden, the organizers, with the Wheels' coach in tow, hurried over to Muck.

They talked briefly, Muck scowling but eventually giving one quick nod of his head. He came back to the Owls and called them all in around him.

"They've a chance to get on the network news apparently," Muck said, unimpressed. "But the television people want to shoot a shootout. You willing to do that?"

It was clear from Muck's expression that he himself didn't want to. But Muck was Muck, never one to force his opinions on others. He was leaving it up to the team.

"You betcha!" said Nish, still beaming from his moment of glory. He couldn't get enough.

"Sure," said Andy.

"Why not?" said Sam.

Muck nodded once, curtly. "Fine, then," he said. "I'll let them know."

The organizers seemed delighted. They immediately cleared the ice of everyone but two camera crews, one on each side of the slot area where the shooters would be coming in. Jeremy and the Wheels' goaltender both took their positions.

The players all went back to their benches while the coaches made up their lists.

Sarah would shoot first.

Travis second.

Nish third.

Muck read down through the entire list. Travis was thrilled. He could feel his heart pounding. He hoped he scored.

Sarah scored easily, a beautiful tuck play as the goalie shot out his stick to poke-check her, and she simply let the puck slide into the net off her backhand.

The big Detroit centre scored on a hard slap-shot that blew right through Jeremy's pads.

The Owls were still congratulating Sarah when Travis, looking down the bench, noticed something very unusual.

Sam, who was far down the list, had her helmet and gloves off and was very carefully pickpocketing Mr. Dillinger's first-aid belt.

She was taking out the scissors.

Muck tapped him on the shoulder. "You're up," he said.

Travis came out onto the ice to a nice round of applause for the winning captain. He loved it. If only the ice surface had been flooded so he could feel that glorious snap and sizzle when he made his turn.

He picked up the puck and wished there was no heavy snow on the ice. He was afraid of losing the puck, and he couldn't stickhandle very quickly. His legs felt funny, like rubber one stride, like lead the next.

Travis came in, faked, went to his backhand, and lifted the puck as hard as he could.

Ping! Off the crossbar.

Travis heard the crowd groan. He slammed his stick in disappointment, but in truth he wasn't that upset. It was just a shootout for fun, after all. It didn't count. And as only hockey players understand, if you're going to miss, the best way is off the crossbar.

As Travis skated back to the bench and his teammates shouted his name, Nish came over the boards.

Right behind Nish, giggling, sat Sam. She held up the scissors in one hand, and raised a thumb with the other.

Sarah was doubled over, laughing so hard tears were coming down her cheeks.

What was going on?

Nish made a grand circle before picking up the puck. It was as if he was on parade. He did some fancy stickhandling and took lots of time.

Both cameras were on him as he came over the blueline. They knew who this was – the kid who had scored the spectacular goal and won the game in overtime – and it was pretty obvious that if any footage made the network news, it was going to be of Nish.

But wait, there was something wrong with Nish's pants! They seemed impossibly low!

Nish tried a fancy sidestep, and his hockey pants dropped right down over his skates.

He tripped and slid helplessly along the ice.

Travis heard two wild squeals of laughter down the bench. Sarah was high-fiving Sam, and Sam was furiously snipping the air with the scissors.

She had cut Nish's suspenders!

Nish was still down, his pants around his ankles, both camera crews zooming in on the overtime hero.

He was going to be on network television.

And only a sweaty pair of boxers had kept him from setting a world record for mooning.

THE END

THE SCREECH OWLS SERIES

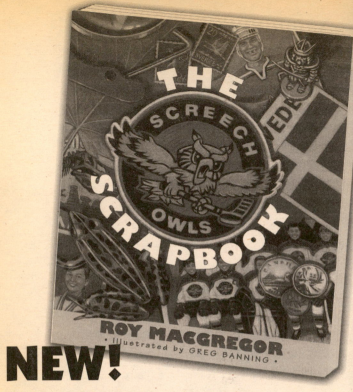

NEW!

THE SCREECH OWLS SCRAPBOOK

by ROY MacGREGOR

Packed with fun, trivia, stats, and background information on the most famous peewee hockey team in the world!

Everything you always wanted to know about the Screech Ow players, Muck, Mr. Dillinger, and highlights from the team's many adventures.

Illustrated in full colour by Screech Owls artist Greg Banning Available now at bookstores everywhere.